ARCHADEA

BARBARA DeFRATIS

authorHOUSE®

AuthorHouse™
1663 Liberty Drive
Bloomington, IN 47403
www.authorhouse.com
Phone: 1 (800) 839-8640

Published by AuthorHouse 12/17/2018

ISBN: 978-1-5462-4360-1 (sc)
ISBN: 978-1-5462-4359-5 (e)

Print information available on the last page.

CONTENTS

PREFACE

Our beloved leader of Norhem, Prime Minister O'Bet Shro, has requested that I write something appropriate in honor of this occasion. The three thousandth anniversary of the deliverance of Norhem and our ally Eas'hem from So'hem (if only the people of Wes'hem would or could understand this fact—that is, if there were any good people there. After all, any fool who would worship a false god like Jeho deserves not only to be deceived but also whatever punishment Our Holy God and Blessed Father, Ablo, will see fit to lay upon them on that Day of Judgment). For what purpose should I write about what is so commonly known, I cannot fathom, but I do suppose it is indeed proper and necessary to do. Even though no true believer and loyal follower of the one and only true deity, Our Holy God and Blessed Father, Ablo, would ever be taken in by the lies and deceptions that either of those unfaithful blasphemers sprouts, some are at least honest enough to call themselves Jehoists. Others call themselves scientists; these have propagated the deception they call *plate tectonics*. Plate tectonics, a fabrication invented by So'hem and their allies, Wes'hem and the Singularity Movement, keeps on resurfacing no matter how many times the *Sacred Book of Ablo* proves otherwise. After all, the ground under our feet is as rock solid as all nine of our shires, which are safe and secure thanks to the blessings of Ablo and our fine and faithful military.

What good and faithful follower of the one true God, Our Holy God and Blessed Father, Ablo would be taken in by their propaganda that the sun is the center point of this so-called solar system and that Archadea is just another planet that rotates around it? Especially considering that Our Holy God and Blessed Father, Ablo, has given to the early saints, to pass down throughout the generations, the truth of how Ablo chose Norhem to be his favored nation and how Ablo not only created Archadea but fathered us all. It is all there in the *Sacred Book of Ablo*, as written by the early saints of our Blessed Ablo. More importantly, for whom; again, I cannot comprehend. Every Norhemian citizen is a good and faithful follower of Our One and Only True God and Blessed Father, Ablo. Every follower must know how Ablo delivered our ancestors from So'hem by his great and mighty fatherly hand, even though Wes'hem, who shares this landmass with us, did turn back and chose to remain allied with So'hem. Even though Our Holy God and Blessed Father, Ablo, delivered us so mightily, So'hem nevertheless was led astray to worship a false god. Even though we share the same orange eyeballs and the same five fingers and thumb, they have chosen to become the red-eyed, blue-haired devils that they are today.

Well, then, If I must, then I must.

FOREWORD

Saint I'Bar, as everyone should know, was one of the few eyewitnesses to this miraculous grand event in our history, the Great Divide. He dared to write about what he had seen, earning himself sainthood. It was such a turning point that we still mark our years BGD/AGD, before or after the Great Divide. The divide changed our world, and our lives, forever.

Three thousand years ago, Our Holy God and Blessed Father delivered Norhem with a mighty quake that caused mountains to rise between Norhem and So'hem. Their demon and his devils fought back, and a fierce battle broke out between them and our Blessed Father Ablo that caused fire and smoke to billow from one of the mountaintops. Thus, all the shires of Norhem were delivered from the evil land of So'hem. Since then, we of Norhem have joined with our brothers and sisters of Eas'hem in a union of peace and harmony to our mutual benefit. We became free to worship the True Deity, our Deliverer, our Holy Father, who blessed all of Archadea with the justly white skin with the vibrant yellow eyes and the honorable green hair, instead of those devious red eyes and vile blue hair. Our Holy God and Blessed Father, Ablo, gave us the sun to light and to warm our days. Once upon a time, those daylight hours, which peaked on the first day of summer with a full thirteen hours of daylight, were all the hours we could work until the blessed invention of electric light. Our Holy God and Blessed Father, Ablo, gave us the four seasons—spring, summer, autumn, and winter, winter starting when the daylight dips down to seven hours on the first day. Our seasons are each five months long, as sure as he gave us his teachings in the *Sacred Book of Ablo*. Our Holy God and Blessed Father, Ablo, gave us the atmosphere to hold in as much warmth as possible, even during the coldest nights of winter, which can get to well below freezing (otherwise known as below zero degrees). Our Holy God and Blessed Father, Ablo, gave us this atmosphere so that the summer days could get as warm as 28 degrees, which is not bad considering that water boils at 100 degrees. Our Holy God and Blessed Father, Ablo, blessed us with the stars to light our nights, giving us time to sleep and providing us with a small taste of how dark and hopeless life without Our Holy God and Blessed Father, Ablo, is like for nonbelievers, even though some have longer days and nights than most, depending on how far north they live. Our Holy God and Blessed Father, Ablo, who created the universe and Archadea in eleven days and rested on the twelfth, thus made the twelfth day genuinely holy.

Our Holy God and Blessed Father, Ablo, still blesses us with spring and autumn, the seasons of transition/renewal and harvest. Our Holy God and Blessed Father, Ablo, has always and will always give us the rain and the snow to grow the food we eat and the Abloton that is spun into the clothes we wear regardless of our class or station in life. Our Holy God and Blessed Father, Ablo, will one day call all the righteous to live in glorious mansions and reign with him for all eternity while the unrighteous serve the righteous for all eternity.

I'Ren Bro
Dean of St. I'Bar College
2980 AGD–3031 AGD

CHAPTER 1
MOVING-IN DAY

"Good morning! In the name of Our Holy God and Blessed Father, Ablo, good morning. I bid a heartfelt welcome to the female members of the class of 3174," a female voice yelled over the loudspeaker. She jokingly added, "Congratulations. You have now successfully navigated your way to the freshmen women's dorm of Saint I'Bar College. Step one on your long journey to higher education is now about to commence."

On this warm and sunny late-summer afternoon, as motor cart after motor cart drove along the uneven brick roads, drivers and passengers bounced around throughout their ride. They finally bounced their way to the underside of the towering emerald-green marble statue of Ablo, with his customary outstretched arms, reaching out as if to hug every person walking around it. This tall, splendid thirty-foot statue was built high on the mound. The figure of Ablo is not only wearing the long, magnificent flowing robes of a bygone era but also looking down on the humbled passersby with longing and love. There, likewise, high above most readers' heads, was also a stone tablet that read, "As Our Holy God and Blessed Father, Ablo, embraces you. He appeals for you to embrace wisdom and understanding as a loving, caring father would. Our Holy God and Blessed Father, Ablo, created all and existed even before time itself did. Our Holy God and Blessed Father, Ablo, appeared on the mound and gave rise to the angel, Jeho, by squeezing him out from his very own loins among the other angels. Not long after this, that thankless angel and son of Our Holy God and Blessed Father, along with a few other angels, did rebel against his Holy Father. However, Ablo's victory was great, even though 74 percent of the angels sided with Jeho. Saddened by this, Ablo decided he needed more company yet again, so this time he pressed yet more seed out of his loins onto the soil up from which all of humanity sprung. Some remained loyal to him while others joined in with Jeho."

Each motor cart was driven in the most orderly fashion, only to pause at the numerous elegantly cut stone steps that led to this seven-storied stone structure, which had been the freshmen ladies' dorm for as long as anyone alive could remember. Each driver stopped and opened the door wide in front of their passengers. For most, it was either a mother or father; for others, it was an aunt or uncle or an occasional grandparent. These freshmen students took two suitcases. Among them was T'Roo Mo.

"Miss T'Roo, if I may, we, the staff, know that you will do well—as well as your older sisters, maybe even better. We are proud of the way you have grown up, almost as proud as the mister and the missus surely must be. We both know they would be here themselves if they were not so busy serving Our Holy God and Blessed Father, Ablo," her humble, soft-spoken driver said.

"Coming through. Excuse me, coming through!" another female freshman said as she plowed past the other freshmen.

"Looks like someone is in an immense hurry to get college started," T'Roo stated as she dusted herself off. She continued, "Where was I? Oh yes, thank you, O'Ron. That means more to me than I can say. But yes, I understand Mother's and Father's busy work schedules. Yes, I understand that they both serve a higher calling than merely being here, just as both my older sisters do. Thank you, again, for seeing me off, and thanks to the rest of my parents' staff for all they have done. I promise to do my best to make everyone proud."

"Well, fare thee well, and may Ablo continue to bless and keep you. What are you talking about? You have already made your family proud just by being accepted here," O'Ron stated with a big, friendly, confident smile. As he prepared to enter the motor cart to drive away, he added, "I wish I could talk with you longer and talk more sense into you, but the longer I stay here, the more trouble I will be in when I get back to the house and someone gets the idea that I am doing something I shouldn't be."

T'Roo replied to herself, "Yes, do the family proud, but don't think too hard about the fact that my parents can more than afford to send me here, as if money does not talk. But does anyone else really care that I am not as intelligent as T'Fra or as business savvy as T'Lee? Does anyone really care that all I want to do is learn to play the Norhemian lyre better so I can play it during religious service? After all, I do not have any five-year plan or anything like that. Today is more than scary enough for me. I do not want to think about tomorrow, and nobody can make me," T'Roo mumbled to herself in protest. She carried both heavy suitcases all the way up the many stone steps that led to two twenty-foot stone columns before the entry doors.

The front desk attendant, who was the voice over the loudspeaker, was only a few years older than the freshmen. "Greetings in the name of Ablo. I am F'Ree Fo, and this is my assistant, D'Con Slo. We are here to assist you by providing whatever support you may need to make it through your freshman year. My first job is to see that everyone gets their room assignments and their own keys to their dorm rooms. Rule number one: Learn to hold on to your key before you lock your door and do not lose your key. Every year, we not only have to use our master key but must make new keys. That is an unnecessary expense that your family can do without, since all that says about you is that you are immature and irresponsible. Now, my assistant's first job is to make sure that no one gets lost on their way to their rooms." All the lights went out, and she added in frustration, "Oh, no! Not again!" Then she quietly reminded herself, *This is these young ladies' first time away from their homes and families; anything could cause them to panic. Relax, ladies, relax. The emergency backup generators will be back on momentarily. There is no reason for anyone to panic. I understand and respect the fact that everyone is accustomed to having their parents or guardians around and being on your own is a new experience. Just remember that this moment of near darkness will pass soon by the grace of Our Holy God and Blessed Father Ablo.* As the lights came back on, F'Ree returned to calling out names while her assistant handed out envelopes, starting with D'Ato Vo's.

"She looks familiar. I know her. I have seen her before. She's the one who was in such a hurry to get college started. I wonder why … I wonder why her family did not drop her off closer to the school," T'Roo pondered aloud as she awaited the mention of her name.

"T'Roo Mo," F'Ree finally called out.

F'Ree handed T'Roo her envelope while D'Con explained, "Your envelope reads that you are in four-seven. That means that you are on the fourth floor, room seven. The other name on the envelope is your roommate, D'Fro Ro. Do you know where that is, or do you need more help?"

"Thank you, but no thank you. I believe I can find it on my own," T'Roo stated as she walked toward the elevator, which was right next to the stairway. She took in a deep breath of relief. She thought, *All praises be to Ablo. There is an elevator, which means I don't have to carry these darn bags all the way up all those floors. If I had to, I think I would die. I would simply die.* She stepped in as others joined her. T'Roo could hear various floors being called out by the elevator operator as she worked the levers and the elevator breaks. The operator took it from the second on up. As the elevator went up, T'Roo and another student stepped out on the fourth floor, but once out of the elevator, they walked off in opposite directions. T'Roo went to the left, while the other went to the right. T'Roo looked down the hallway as she began walking to her dorm room. "Oh, great, just great. There is no way to walk on this stone tile without every step echoing throughout the hallway. I suppose I could take my shoes off, but with only socks on, I imagine these stone tiles would become almost as slippery as ice." T'Roo passed many portraits of Saint I'Bar, each one with a verse from the *Holy Book of Ablo*.

"I don't believe it. How few changes of clothes am I to endure?" one student screamed out from one of the rooms that T'Roo passed.

"Relax, we will have the option of either having more clothes brought here or buying more clothes later in the school year. We will need to do so when the season's changes. At least both our families had the forethought to have our evening wear shipped here and hung up before today."

Presumably her roommate reassured her, as she replied, "Yes, I am grateful this is one less thing to worry about."

Oh, well, where was I? T'Roo thought. *Wow, I guess I have been more blessed than I realized. It seems that my parents did the same thing, as tonight's evening wear has already been hung up. I guess this is the blessing of being the youngest. My parents made all their mistakes with my older sisters. I suppose high expectations are the price they had to pay for their experience. Well, at least I can't say that I am all that stressed out—yet. The question is, should I be grateful or disappointed that my dorm room is at the end of this long hallway? Maybe I am more pampered than I realized, but all this additional walking will add up by the end of the academic year. Then again, since it is one of the two rooms right in front of the patio, no matter what happens with the electricity, I will always be able to find it. It is just a matter of walking all the way to it. I should not forget that the best thing about those patios is the glass doors that lead to them. There is not only fresh air and natural lighting but also something to focus on other than all these darn portraits, whose eyes I can almost feel watching me. In time, I guess I will get used to it. Maybe I'll even get over it, I hope. Oh, well, at least there is carpeting by both halves of the patio, and there is only a brick wall between both halves of the patio and not more portraits.*

T'Roo finally reached her dorm room. She slowly peeked in to see that it was just as shallow and just as wide as her older sister had described it. From the doorway, she read her full name on the one closet curtain, D'Fro Ro on the other. From there, she looked in and saw both beds, which were already made and labeled accordingly. Under the one bed, she saw a person reading a book. As she approached, the other side of the room came into view. Now she could see under each raised bed; there was a desk, desk lamp, typewriter, and space to study. Those were the things her older sisters had told her about, exactly where her sisters said they would be. Also, there was the anticipated five-drawer dresser, small bookcase, and glowing picture of Ablo quoting from his Sacred Book.

"Greetings. Who are you? If you are not T'Roo Mo, then you had better get out of here!" the person stated, lifting her head from her book long enough to notice she was no longer alone in the room.

"Well then, it looks as if I can stay, since I am <u>T'Roo</u>. D'Fro Ro, I presume? May I ask what you are reading, since no class has even come close to starting?" T'Roo answered.

"Why, yes, I am, and I can prove it. As far as what I am reading, I am studying the map of the college. Getting lost is not on my list of things to do at college. The question is, can you?" D'Fro stated.

"Yes, I can," replied T'Roo. She showed her room assignment card and in turn was shown D'Fro's card.

All too quickly, D'Fro resumed her chattering. "In that case, I am certainly pleased to meet you. Hopefully and prayerfully, by the grace of Our Holy God and Blessed Father, Ablo, we will both be here for a full year, so we might as well learn to get along. My major is the Ministry of Elementary Education so that I can follow in my mother's footsteps— or, rather, the steps she took until she got married. I know. I really should be looking forward to getting married and raising a family, but since there is no man in my life, I think—I hope—that Our Holy God and Blessed Father, Ablo, will not only understand but also bless me as I pursue my career choice since it is really for his glory. My older sister is already assisting her husband in building his family's business into an even more successful business, as a good help-mate should do. Have you chosen a proper ladylike major, or are you here to find a husband who can be groomed into a good provider?" D'Fro asked in full yellow-eyed wonder.

"No, I am not here to get married; nor have I chosen a major yet. My independent study is on the Norhemian lyre. I guess that means I should eventually be majoring in the Music Ministry," T'Roo sheepishly answered, fearing she might and up regretting saying anything on the subject. As she began to unpack, she quickly added, "Did you happen to notice how nicely our beds were made? I have two older sisters who attended St. I'Bar, and they warned me that the staff only makes the bed the night before we move in. From here on out, it is our responsibility, until the last day of class. I don't know about you, but I can only hope to keep this bed as nice as it is now."

D'Fro began to provide more boring details about her family as T'Roo continued to unpack and do her best to listen—or at least pretend to. *No wonder we have been assigned to each other. Her family is just like mine. Oh my God, is my family this boring too? Oh, my God, it probably is*, thought T'Roo, who finally finished her unpacking. She asked, "Did you have a chance to see the gardens? I hear they are not only the most colorful but also the most beautiful in West Shire. There are even a few rare trees that can only be found here on this campus."

"No, I have not. Why should I?" D'fro snapped back. "My family was blessed enough to send me to college to get a degree, not to become a gardener or a member of the cleaning staff. Have you not yet learned? Even though we will have the responsibilities of making our beds and cleaning our room, thanks to the blessings of Ablo, we are above the petty concerns of these mere workers. Do not forget, we are here because we have a higher calling."

"Well, I don't know about you, but I could use the breath of fresh air," T'Roo stated. As she prepared to step out, she timidly added, "A nice walk would do me good. I take it that you would prefer not to join me."

"You are correct. After all, tonight is the Freshmen Dinner. I have better things to do. I have prayers and meditations to do to prepare myself for it, not to mention clothes. You should be doing the same. After all, just because our evening clothes were pre-hung for us, we should not presume all the wrinkles were removed. That is, if you know what's good for you. After all, as they say, clothes not only reveal the person but say so much about the person. That's all assuming you really came here with the intent of making your family proud," D'fro stated in all her self-righteous glory. T'Roo simply and quietly left.

Oh my, just as I thought. All I can hear are my footsteps and those of others still walking around on these stone tiles, T'Roo thought as she walked to the stairway and down the steps. She neither had anything to carry that would have prevented her from taking the stairs nor was in any mood to risk meeting up with another D'Fro.

In one of the many smaller garden patches, T'Roo saw an older woman wearing light taupe peasant Abloton work clothes, along with a taupe headscarf, which served the dual purpose of keeping her hair clean and out of her eyes while she worked. She, in turn, saw T'Roo, wearing her middle-class bleached light blue Abloton, smartly decorated with thin dark blue stripes that ran down each sleeve and pant leg. Her long green hair occasionally blew in her face.

"Good morning. My name is T'Roo Mo. What is your name?" she asked with an outstretched hand and a friendly smile that seemed to stretch from ear to ear.

"I don't think that you really want to do that. My hands are too dirty. But thank you anyway for your most kind and generous offer. My name is K'Ree, miss, just K'Ree. By your clothes, I see you are one of the students here. Why would you want to know my name? Usually, students don't want to know my name. Most students and faculty simply want to know what kind of flowers I'm planting or the quickest way from here to there. If I am acknowledged at all, it is a simple gardener who is not worthy of notice, because there are so many of us working poor people around," she tearfully responded.

"Yes, this does go against Our Holy God and Blessed Father, Ablo's, holy and righteous system of rewards and punishments, which I do know of and truly respect and honor. Then again, why not ask you your name? At least you know what you are doing, why you are here, and that you belong here," T'Roo explained. She added with a forced smile, "All I know is that since my parents can afford to send me here,

I have a higher calling, whatever that means translated in Norhemian. I wish I knew how to explain that I have this Norhemian lyre, which I wish I could play far better than I do. That tree looks beautiful. I remember seeing something like it in an old painting, depicting a time when there were far more trees than there are now. Norhem must have been very charming back then, not that our Norhem is ugly now. Speaking of these flowers, they are gorgeous. If only I knew more about them, especially how to grow them."

"These flowers are edelweiss. They come in all these many shades of blue, violet, red, yellow, and orange, such as these. Some are darker, while others are lighter. It usually depends on how healthy they are. But they are all so fragile, except for the white ones. These white flowers are the resilient ones, as they can seem to handle any weather. I imagine they could survive just about anything. Oh, and this tree is the Norhemian fir, which was once very common along the mountain range that divides Norhem from So'hem, but the people had other needs at the time. As a result of more trees being chopped down than new ones planted, they are still very few and far between," K'ree explained as she continued to tend to them. She quietly followed T'Roo's lead, until she added, "Hold it, young lady! Why are you wasting your valuable time chitchatting about flowers? Shouldn't you be getting ready for that Freshmen Dinner of yours?"

"Yes, I know the drill. The Freshmen Dinner is where we get all dressed up to meet and greet not only our fellow freshmen but also influential upperclassmen who can mentor us. Even more importantly, we will meet our professors, who can make us or break us. This dinner is my one and only chance to make a good first impression, to make my family proud of me," T'Roo said with her eyes rolling, like a person who has been lectured on this subject too many times. A mystified T'Roo asked, "What would you know about the Freshmen Dinner? After all, aren't students the only ones who ever had to endure it—along with the teaching staff, of course?"

"Never mind. Let's just say that word gets around. Just do your best, relax, and be yourself, and you will do just fine," K'ree explained as she picked a few white edelweisses. "Why don't you go to that dinner like the white edelweiss, which can survive and thrive through anything? Wear these in your hair, and they just might inspire you to wow everyone in the room. If not, perhaps they could brighten up that dorm room of yours. If I remember hearing correctly, those rooms are so uniformly identical that one might compare it to living in a factory. After all, as it is written in the *Sacred Books of Ablo*, we are all different yet the same, since we all serve Our Holy God and Blessed Father, Ablo," K'Ree said as she sent T'Roo on her way back to her dorm room.

*   *   *

Meanwhile, at the prime minister's palace, the prime minister's private secretary asked, "Sir, excuse me, sir. I am very sorry for this interruption, but the High Cleric O'Lam is here and would like to have a word with you, sir, in private. He would like to know if now is a good time or if he should come back when it is more convenient. What should I tell him?"

"He is the high cleric. Tell him to come in," Prime Minister E'Li ordered. He turned to the high cleric and said, "I bid you welcome. And to what do I owe the honor of this visit?"

"Why is it so dark in here?" the high cleric asked.

"I like it dark sometimes. It allows me to be alone with my thoughts. But since you are here, permit me to turn on the lights," the prime minister said.

"Thank you, Prime Minister E'Li. If it is alright with you, I was hoping we could talk about few concerns, but first, the upstart who is attempting to compete with the church in feeding the hungry, which we cannot have. After all, if they can go someplace else to eat, all too many will do so. As a result, their bodies will be fed, but their souls will be left to starve to death. We must not allow this that to happen," the high cleric stated.

"Yes, I agree completely. Consider the matter handled," Prime Minister E'Li stated. "And the other matters would be?"

"How is the new power plant progressing?" the high cleric asked.

"From my last report, I am pleased to say that it is progressing very well. In fact, there is the most excellent chance, if things continue as they are, that the new mega-power plant will be operational ahead of schedule. The Grand Opening ceremony is set for the first day of autumn and will be very much a part of our Festival of the Lights celebration," the prime minister boasted.

"Good, excellent. The truth of the matter is I am still hearing some questions on whether this new power plant will actually solve the problem. Currently we have a power plant every two miles, but power outages have not only continued but increased annually," the high cleric questioned.

"You can rest assured, High Cleric, I have been assured by not only the top scientists and best engineers of Norhem but also by the preeminent architects and the finest builders that this power plant, which they worked on, is the new standard. This power plant is more powerful than all the others put together, and when this one is connected to the others, they will generate so much power that people will soon forget what power outages were."

"That is the most excellent news. I will pass that on. After all, the church has not only a vested interest in seeing that all the reading lights can remain on but also a monetary interest so we can continue to afford feeding the hungry. Farmland is at such a premium. What can I say? The sooner the church receives our return on investment, the sooner we can see that the knowledge and love of Our Holy God and Blessed Father, Ablo, can truly cover this land. Sadly, far too many families do not yet love Our Holy God and Blessed Father, Ablo, with all their hearts and souls. They are in danger of going to that unspeakable place of punishment. We, the spiritual leaders of Norhem, must do everything in our power to keep them from being lured away from the true faith, lest Our Holy God and Blessed Father, Ablo, hold us accountable if any choose eternal damnation over eternal life," the high cleric explained.

"Yes, High Cleric, sir. I am aware of the burdens you must bear. That is why I have continued the many traditions my predecessors have started. I have ensured taxation is not among the many burdens you and your church face. We aim to aid you in every way humanly possible in your divine mission, to save the souls of each and every person in Norhem," the prime minister stated. "Who knows? If this venture is successful enough, we may even convince many a So'hemian to come over to our side, the right side."

CHAPTER 2
THE FRESHMEN DINNER

The nervous freshmen class slowly meandered into the dining hall. The first room they were called to was the side dining room, which was usually opened up only when the main dining hall got too full. But this evening it was open.

"Come in, come in. Our photographer will take your picture while his assistant collects your fingerprints. The photographs and fingerprinting are both security measures for your own safety. If everyone cooperates, it will take no time at all," the gentleman stated.

Their hushed voices joined with all the other hushed conversations, blending into a beehive-like hum. They soon formed a line to get the photo taken, then walked over to get fingerprinted, where they were handed moist disposable towelettes to prevent dirtying their clothes. They continued to mingle. Some were meeting for the first time, while others were childhood friends, and still others were only passing acquaintances who had met once or twice previously. Meanwhile, the dinner guests just passed the workers, who were busily trading in burnt-out bulbs for working ones, but also the ones coming and going from the basement, where each building's backup generator was located. These freshmen students were all dressed in their the court of best, from the ladies' most excellent and colorfully expensive Abloton pantsuits to the men's equally affluent and colorful formal dress skirt suits. They were each handed a program. T'Roo was dressed in her most beautiful violet and red pantsuit, and she had decorated her hair with the white edelweiss that the gardener had given her for luck rather than the silver and gold threads that enhance most of the girls' hair.

As the freshmen and the others meandered to the tables, T'Roo soon found herself assigned to one of the freshmen tables, designated for females only. Once again, she met D'Ato, D'Lir, and L'Rom. From her side of the table, T'Roo could see and hear her fellow classmates exchange greetings. Her mind roamed the room, from the upperclassmen's table to the table of professors and various honored guests, whose identity T'Roo could only guess at, according to the program and their dress.

"Attention, attention! Ladies and gentlemen, honored guests: D'Ma Cho, the oldest daughter of the prime minister of our beloved nation, Norhem, who is here with her husband, businessman Mr. Cho, and the minister of West Shire since Saint I'Bar College, is the ordained center of higher education for the community of West Shire, E'Lo Dro, who is here with his wife, Mrs. Cho. Now, if I may continue to have your attention, I am Chief of Campus Security, Officer K'Too Ko. Professor O'Well Thro, the host for this year's Freshmen Dinner, is about to lead us all in the opening prayer so we may get this year's dinner started. Now, I request that all present rise to their feet in honor of the opening prayer."

The graying blue-haired soldier was dressed in her military best. T'Roo recognized her as the person who was handing out the programs. The gray-haired scholarly gentleman reverently walked up to the microphone and began his most reverent chant. "This is the day. This is the hour that Our Holy God and Blessed Father, Ablo, has made. Let the heavens rejoice and all of Norhem be glad in it, be glad in it." The others repeated, twice, in equal reverence, except for Officer K'Too, who was busily studying all their mannerisms. He concluded with "Let West Shire worship Ablo's Holy Name. Let all the people of Norhem worship Ablo's Holy Name. One day, all of Archadea will worship Our Holy God and Blessed Father, Ablo's Holy Name, and all the heavens will truly and fully rejoice and be glad on that Holy Day. So be it, Ablo, so be it." The others again repeated twice before sitting down.

*   *   *

The gardener, K'Ree, was among the many working poor who humbly walked up to the twenty-foot solid wood doors and struggled to open them. This was the only way into the church building. The first rooms they passed were the cloakrooms, where they hung up their coats and hats. From there, they entered and passed through the sanctuary, with its hundred-foot arched ceilings and many painted glass windows. They passed by the sanctuary pews, which were reserved for those who could afford them. Since these were the working poor, they headed straight to the commoner's pews in the back, as a pre-meal church service was about to begin. An assistant cleric entered. All in attendance rose to their feet as he continued to walk back. He motioned for them to sit down.

"Before the beginning of time, there was Ablo. Our Holy God and Blessed Father, Ablo, birthed many a divine son and many daughters, including one Jeho, by way of his own seed, and that son later led the rebellion against his father. After that act of treason, Jeho was kicked out of paradise and to Kur, where he now rules, awaiting his divine judgment. As sure as the entrance to Kur is located at the foot of the Zageris Mountain range, which divides Norhem from So'hem, the true believers and wise saints know better than to be seen around places of evil and temptation, such as the Zageris Mountain range, for they know and understand that one day, Our Holy God and Blessed Father, Ablo, will flatten that mountain range and seal all who dwell within forever and ever. Then, all of Archadea will live in peace and tranquility." The cleric added, "Sobeit, Sobeit, but for now, we must ask all who dwell here to affirm their loyalty to Our Holy God and Blessed Father, Ablo, in a time in which he can still be found. I ask all who wish to affirm their loyalty to Our Holy God and Blessed Father, Ablo, who also gave birth to our ancestors, to continue spreading his good seed in the soil, Sobeit, along with me."

"Sobeit, Sobeit, Sobeit," all repeated in unison.

"For the food that we are about to consume, we thank you, Our Holy God and Blessed Father, Ablo," the cleric stated, but instead of continuing straight to the altar, they went right to the worn -out basement steps that led to the charity kitchen, where the shiny white marble floor of the sanctuary had now been replaced with an old, worn -out rug. K'Ree was behind another woman in line, who whispered her name to O'Ron too softly for K'Ree to recognize what name was given. Everyone heard his response.

"How dare you come here to be fed when you missed as many days of work as you have missed?" O'Ron stated.

"But you don't understand. My mother was sick. I needed to take care of her," the woman begged.

"No, it is you who does not understand. Our Holy God and Blessed Father, Ablo, permits only those who have sinned against him in thought, word, or deed to get sick. If your mother sinned, you should have left her to suffer, since that suffering would have led to her repentance," O'Ron stated. "This is yet another way that sin gets spread out: first, your mother's sin leads to her sickness, which leads to your sin of laziness, by not going to work. Others see that you have stayed home, and they stay home with their own tedious excuses. As if Our Holy God and Blessed Father, Ablo, would feed someone who has not earned their own daily bread. Get back in the sanctuary and beg his forgiveness, and maybe, just maybe, you will get at least a glass of water. Next!" O'Ron ordered.

"Greetings, and you are?" said the volunteer, whose nametag read O'Ron.

"I am K'Ree," she said softly.

"K'Ree, yes, I have you right here," O'Ron stated. He pointed to her name on the list. "I also see a son listed with you. May I ask where he is and why he is not with you?"

"He is not with me because he found a job and is working late. I am hoping and praying by the grace of Our Holy God and Blessed Father, Ablo, that he will either be fed there or paid enough money to afford to pay for his own food."

"Sobeit, Sobeit," O'Ron, K'Ree, and others responded in unison.

"Well then, since you know that we have you on record as a good worker, you may receive one meal and one bag of food as your thanks for your service. Next!" O'Ron commanded as K'Ree walked away.

* * *

Back at the freshman dinner, the meal was being served by the kitchen staff. The rest of her table companions had finally noticed T'Roo. They introduced themselves, but with a table this size, there were too many names to remember. It was the same old song and dance: some of their parents were in business, while others were in the ministry or politics.

D'Lir remained noticeably silent about her family, leaving T'Roo grateful that she was not the only one who preferred not to talk about her family. T'Roo and D'Lir were the first ones to finish their meals. D'Lir wandered off, while T'Roo headed off to the ballroom in the vain hope that the evening might improve. Sadly, as T'Roo entered the ballroom, there was neither music to encourage anyone to dance nor a friendly mood, just formal stuffiness. As she walked from window to window, more and more people gradually entered the ballroom. T'Roo decided it was time for her to get into the meet and greet. Like it or not, this was what they expected of her. Soon, T'Roo saw D'Lir wandering back in.

"Where did you wander off to, and why didn't you invite me?" T'Roo asked.

"I thought there were other rooms to explore. Unfortunately, I was wrong. All the other doors are locked. We stuck here until we are told that we can leave—like it or not," D'Lir stated. "Sounds like we had better learn to make the best of this situation. The best to you. Wish me luck too," T'Roo said. She began wandering from conversation to conversation, catching bits and pieces of many. All too many began with "My father is" or "My mother is" or even "My older brother or sister is." These turned into the most boring conversations, so she quickly learned to escape as soon as they began.

"I play the alto fife," one of the female students said.

"Excellent. I play the Nohemian fife. The Saint I'Bar Concert Band is always looking for new band members," one of the female upperclasspersons said.

"Oh, yes, I almost forgot. There are college bands, so if there are bands, then there are also ensembles, especially string ensembles. I play a Norhemian lyre. How does one go about joining an existing string ensemble or forming a new one?" T'Roo asked with great excitement.

"I am sorry, but I play in the marching band. I am here to beat the concert band to the best musicians. The only thing I know about the various ensembles, be they the woodwind or string or percussion, is that they have the same problem as the bands, namely, musicians graduating out of them. If I were you, I would check with the Music Ministry to see if there are any string ensembles looking for the lyre that you play," a male upper-class person said. "By the way," he added, "if you happen to know anyone who plays a band instrument, I would deeply appreciate it if you could point them out to me, especially if they play well."

"I'm very sorry. I can't say I know anybody here that well. I wish I did, but I don't. After all, you have been most helpful," T'Roo said.

"By the way, I play bass drum in the marching band. May I ask what the differences are between the alto lyre, the Norhemian lyre, and the bass lyre? I have heard them talked about, but that is all I know about them," he said.

"Well, the alto lyre has eight strings, while the Norhemian lyre has twelve, two of each of the six strings which are why both the lead and the backup accompanies the alto lyres which play the leads. Not only that, but also the alto lyre has a higher range than the Norhemian lyre, but the Norhemian lyre has lower notes than the alto. Well, the bass lyre is self-explanatory. All of its notes are on the bass scale, which leaves the Norhemian lyre to play the chords in between the two of them. In a string ensemble, there are the lead alto lyre and the backup alto lyre, along with the lead Norhemian lyre and the backup Norhemian lyre. Having a lead and a backup adds volume to both the alto lyres and the Nohemian lyres," T'Roo answered.

"Thank you for clearing that up. Now, if you will excuse me, I must find out how many future marching band members are here before the concert band takes all the best ones," he said before walking away, leaving T'Roo to continue her wanderings as well.

"Professor O'Mar Chvo is not here. Well, now we know who wears the skirt in his family," one of the middle-aged gentlemen joked.

Soon, T'Roo found herself following some other students in meeting and greeting Professor O'Well. "Greetings to one and all. As you all know, I am Professor O'Well Thro. I am one of two professors here to introduce you to the sciences. As you all should know by now, it was Our Holy God and Blessed Father, Ablo, who proclaimed through his prophets and saints in his infinite wisdom that no one should study the sciences without a firm foundation of faith. That is why faith is taught throughout the primary and secondary levels of education while the sciences are taught in college. Here you will have ample opportunity to go as far as your mental skills will take you—as long as you do not wander off from Ablo's goodwill."

A male student began, "My father is …"

This was T'Roo's cue to exit as fast as she could, unless she wanted to know whether his father was as dull as her father. She soon found herself in another conversation.

"If this is so, I do not know what to call it. I wish we got our class schedules this morning instead of tomorrow morning. I don't know what anyone else thinks about this dinner, but I, for one, would rather focus on the professors I'll be having than waste my time in this meet-and-greet in the vain attempt to impress someone I may never see again," complained one female student. T'Roo recognized her as D'Ato, one of the few students with yellow eyes and curly green hair who did not adorn her hair in silver or gold.

"Well, you know why it is done this way, don't you?" a male student jumped in.

"No, why don't you enlighten us, oh wise one," another male student responded.

"Okay, then, I will. The college does this so we will all be forced to talk with all the professors," he explained, unaffected by the previous remark.

A female student threw out an explanation, tempting other students to comment. "I have heard rumors that this is done so the chief of security officer has a chance to see if any students and professors are already too familiar with each other. If there are any such cases, then security knows who to question first—about who met whom, when, and where."

T'Roo's curiosity gets the better of her. "Why would security worry about that? After all, isn't that why we are here, to meet and greet all the professors who will recommend us along the way?"

"Security is looking for people to make mistakes and give themselves away so they can observe which students and professors are secret members of the Singularity Movement." This came from the same dark-blue-haired student with silver threads. Her orange eyes were wide open as she eagerly speculated.

V'To jumped into the conversation, searching for agreement. "Well, if there are any traitors here, I don't care who they are or who they think they are. If they are part of that traitorous Singularity Movement, then they need to get caught by Our Holy God and Blessed Father, by Ablo's grace, so they can be openly arrested and swiftly and justly dealt with. The sooner the better so that we can be left alone in peace. After all, we all know that the whole point of the Singularity Movement is to deceive as many Norhemians and Wes'hemians as possible into siding with those So'hemians, who worship that false god of theirs, so they can destroy the Norhemian way of life. Everyone knows that those So'hemians are only here to kill and destroy all that is good and holy, which is why they hate us so very much."

A male student spoke next. "I don't know if that is the real truth or not or just the party line, but I do know one thing. I think we have begun to draw the attention of Officer K'Too Ko. I suggest that we slowly and calmly disperse lest we confirm her probable suspicions. Remember, no one make any quick movements, and most certainly do not make any eye contact with anyone, especially Officer K'Too Ko herself. The life that you save will be your own. So let us all, very slowly and calmly, walk away from each other," he whispered as he also made sure that he made absolutely no visible eye contact with Officer K'Too.

As Officer K'Too stepped into the center of the ballroom with microphone in hand, she called out, "Attention, attention! I have been advised to tell you that it is time to end this evening's activity. After all, tomorrow is your orientation day, and most, if not all, of you will be needing to purchase additional supplies. Some of you may want to take advantage of the fact that the bookstore doors open at four in the morning. That is three hours before the first breakfast will be served."

"Yes, that is good advice, since the lines at the bookstore have always been notoriously long. Those who have made it in early have always made it out early," Professor I'Var Fro advised.

"Thank you, Professor, "Officer K'Too said. "Professor I'Var Fro has been kind enough to volunteer to lead us in the sending prayer. But first, let me remind everyone once again that these very doors will open at exactly seven in the morning. First breakfast will be served, and then every student is expected to be here on time and to pick up their own—and only their own—schedule. We have had problems in the past when others have asked a friend to pick up their schedules for them. Between the schedule not getting to the person on time and giving that person enough time to get into mischief, the college has put a complete stop to that practice; however, within every class, there is at least one person who attempts to get away with it. Now, do not be late to any of your classes tomorrow, or else!" she added before she handed the microphone to him. "Professor, if you will be so kind to lead the departing prayer."

Professor I'Var began to lead the chant in unison. "Ablo, Our Holy God and Blessed Father, dismiss us with your blessings, we pray. Fill our hearts and fill our minds with peace and joy and rest. Let us, your submissive children, depart triumphantly in obedient love, according to your goodwill as Our Holy God and Blessed Father, the one and only True God of gods. Sobeit, Our Holy God and Blessed Father, Ablo, Sobeit."

Everyone prepared to leave. They once again sounded like the hum of bees as they murmured their farewells, congratulating each other for an evening well spent. Everyone who attended or was invited, that is. The workers who had cleaned up the dining hall now had the job of cleaning up the ballroom as well.

CHAPTER 3
THE BRIEFING

Not long after F'Ree entered the prime minister's palace, she was greeted by his private secretary.

"Miss F'Ree Fo, you are late and the last one to report," the private secretary sternly stated.

"Yes, I am very sorry, but I got this flat tire, which I was left alone to change," F'Ree began.

"Spare me your sob story. I have no time for it; nor do I care. The care and maintenance of your motor cart is your responsibility, not mine, as sure as it is your responsibility to navigate your way here as speedily as possible. I will simply inform the prime minister that you are finally here. You might as well have a seat. Our prime minister is indeed a very busy man. There is no assurance that the prime minister will be able to find the time for you as quickly as you would like him to, since it would appear that you have no respect for his time." As he stood up to walk away, she couldn't help but notice how tall this private secretary was. She suddenly started missing the old one, who was so much shorter than herself. She sat down on one of the hard wooden side chairs next to the desk, where she read his nameplate, "E'Lam

Cho," and wondered if he was somehow related to the prime minister's daughter. This turned into a pleasant distraction for F'Ree, since it kept her from feeling all too small in this rather grandly majestic private office, which permitted no one to look in, except for the prime minister himself.

The private secretary walked back in and announced as he held the door open for her, "The prime minister will see you now." F'Ree Fo walked into what appeared to be the kind of office even the highest paid Norhemian executive could only dream to afford. This office not only had many expensive, highly decorated lamps but also fewer windows than the laws required, since the law demanding office activities to be visible applied to private offices only, likewise exempting church offices. This elegant government office also had the most expensive wallpaper and flooring, including three glass windows nearly floor to ceiling in height and surrounded by only the most exquisitely decorative curtains, which were all under a finely painted ceiling mural. There, sitting at his desk, which was taller, wider, deeper, and mostly decorated in gold leaf, its size and elegance highlighted by the three very tall windows behind it, which is no doubt made up of one-way glass, was the prime minister.

"Greetings, Prime Minister, sir. May I say that you are indeed a very courageous man to be standing right in front of the window to look out it when you surely must know that all of So'hem would love to see to you dead and buried along with everything you stand for," F'Ree said flirtatiously.

"Thank you, but to be honest, you give me far too much credit. This window, like the other two windows, is made out of one-way bulletproof glass. There is no way anyone can do me harm while I stand here. Thanks to Our Holy

God and Blessed Father, Ablo, who gave our scientists this technology," the prime minister said jokingly. Then, in a serious tone, he added, "So, you must be F'Ree Fo, since everyone else has already given their reports. You must be here to report on how the Freshmen Dinner went from St. I'Bar College from the female perspective, the college of West Shire, since every other college representatives from every other shire, has come and gone already. Even the man who represents the freshmen males has not only filed his report but has already left. I was expecting you well over a half-hour ago. Pray tell, what took you so long?"

"Well, suit yourself, but if you should change your mind, feel free to have a seat," he said and added, "So why don't we just get right to business. Is there anyone at St. I'Bar College, be they student or professor whom we should be concerned about?"

"Mr. Prime Minister, before the dinner, I studied and reviewed everything on the list to look for to indicate a spy in the room. But at the dinner, I saw none of that behavior acted out. Yes, all the freshmen were nervous, but no one particularly was more nervous than anyone else. After all, they are freshmen. This is, for most if not all, their first time away from their homes and families. That does not mean, however, that I will not be keeping an eye on anyone. After all, they all are still potential traitors to Norhem and Our Holy God and Blessed Father, Ablo," F'Ree explained.

"So I heard. Thank you for your report and your confirmation. I trust if anything should change, you will inform me with greater speed and urgency than your arrival here. After all, I believe that you indeed do understand: the quicker we can isolate and start gathering up the evidence on those So'hemian spies, the less damage they can inflict on the good people of Norhem," Prime Minister E'Li said.

"Yes, Mr. Prime Minister, sir. Thank you. I am indeed humbled by your vote of confidence. I shall count it as high praise and work that much harder to prove that it is well placed indeed," F'Ree responded.

"Thank you for your service, and good evening. I trust that you will have a safe drive home." He pointed to the door that his private secretary was holding open.

"Good evening, indeed, sir," F'Ree responded.

As she walked out, a messenger walked in.

"The arrest has been made, and the prisoner is now into custody in accordance with the law," the messenger said.

As soon as she was gone, D'Ma stepped out of the shadows and said, "Thank you, Father, for at least attempting to keep this report nice and short. After all, F'Ree was indeed completely honest. The freshman dinner at St. I'Bar College was a nicely boring one, even though the excuse for her tardiness was weak to say the least."

"Stop right there. I have no reason to question F'Ree's loyalty. This is the first time she has been late. If she keeps on being late, then I will place her under watch, but only then," the Prime Minister said.

"As you wish, Father, Mister Prime Minister, sir, but as I was saying about the dinner, I kept looking for any sign of something, anything, that might be suspicious, but between those who were so worried about getting ahead in their field of interest and those who were scared stiff of being away from their mommy and daddy, no one dared to conspire with anyone about anything. Thus begs the question: What was that arrest all about?" D'Ma said.

"We caught a man attempting to form a group that was about to compete against the church in the feeding of the hungry. As you are well aware, such activity is against the law, since no one is permitted to compete against the church in any way, shape, or form. After all, only the church is permitted to save souls," he explained. He added, "Good, let us pray to Our Holy God and Blessed Father, Ablo, that the students and faculty at all the colleges, especially Saint I'Bar College, stay that way so I can remain Norhem's prime minister for yet another term."

"Which reminds me, now that your workday is finally over with, can I finally take my newly wedded husband home?" D'Ma asked.

"Yes, E'Lam, you are dismissed. In fact, since you have worked so long today, would you prefer to come in an hour or so later tomorrow, or take an extra-long lunch?"

*   *   *

In the So'hemian palace, their king sat in his private study, full of antiques passed down from the many So'hemian kings that came before, busts and portraits in gold trim like the gold that trimmed the walls, floors, ceiling, and even the thick heavy curtains there to secure his privacy, which would have been outlawed anywhere else. There he took a deep, relaxing breath, knowing that tomorrow was another day and he must remain in control to secure not only his power but his well-being.

"Greeting in the name of the one and only Blessed God above all other gods, Jeho," said an older woman dressed in long, flowing religious robes as she stepped out of the dark doorway into the room. "Is the anything the matter, good

King A'Mar XX, whom we hope and pray that our Blessed God, Jeho, shall continue to bestow with his good favor?"

"No, not really. It just feels good to get off of the royal throne and sit on a simple chair. With all due respect, what brings the high priestess herself out and about at here at this late hour? I hope the church is not experiencing any dire emergency, other than the usual power outages," the graying king said, half in jest, as he reflected upon his most decorated crown sitting on his desk.

"It is rather interesting that you should mention power outages. After all, we are finally getting over a winter in which So'hem had the most power outages on record, as less daylight always leads to more reading lights, especially among our elder citizens, one of whom I am rapidly becoming. I know because my old reading lamp has since become too dim to use. I had to replace it with one that could take a brighter bulb, which means next winter will be even worse than this one, since we all will be one year older with even more limits on our capacities and abilities. I fear, despite the fact that we have built a power plant every two miles, if we continue to have power outages much longer, it will become impossible to continue blaming those blasphemous Norhemians for them. Your Highness, you must know that must do something before the people begin to question your authority, or even worse, revolt," she probed.

"Yes, I am. From what I hear, Norhem is in the process of building a massive power plant. Their leaders are promising it will solve all their energy problems," King A'Mar XX Shra said.

"Will that solve our problems as well?" Priestess Z'Raa questioned.

"Possibly. After all, I have spies watching the construction of this power plant of theirs as well as scientists who are studying their activity. From what my science and engineering experts have told me, we have two options at least, with a possible third. Personally, I fail to see how sabotaging them will help us. There are two serious selections on the table that my counselors and I are still talking over. We can either copy their plans—that is, if they are worth duplicating—or we can channel some of the power from their new power plant and let them solve our outrage problem for us."

Priestess Z'Raa thought about this a moment. "Well, either action would be most proper. Need I remind the king of So'hem that our God, Jeho, made everything, and therefore, everything is his and what is his also belongs to those who call upon his name. All things taken into consideration, there are more wages of sin than mere death, and the most grievous sin of them all is idolatry. The lowest form of idolatry is worshiping a false god, as those Norhemians do."

"Unfortunately, that does not answer the question of which one we should choose," the king said. "After all, it is indeed doubtful that the people of Norhem would agree with you. They would resist and fight us if they even suspected what we are contemplating. The very last thing we want is a real war against Norhem."

"As long as you remember that you are So'hem's king, whose God is indeed the one and only Blessed God above all other gods, Jeho, and the one and only who truly created all of Archadea and all that is, was, or ever will be. Then you will have the courage and wisdom to do what needs to be done. But yet do not be too involved personally, my king.

After all, should this plan fail, you may need to deny any knowledge of it."

"Fear not, my good high priestess. My experts have everything under control, and they have guaranteed the success of this endeavor. Nevertheless, should this plan fail in any way, which is highly unlikely, we already have someone ready, willing, and able to take any and all blame, as long as we take good care of his widowed mother, which we plan to do," he said.

"With that, all our businesses have been concluded. That is all that I can say, Letitbeso," the priestess said.

"Letitbeso, and thank you for reminding me, Priestess," King A'Mar said as they bid each other farewell.

CHAPTER 4
ORIENTATION DAY

The freshmen students were woken up by the morning call-to-worship bell. Each student had been trained well to repeat the morning chant three times, even T'Roo and D'Fro, who did their chant in unison. "All good, faithful, obedient, and fruitful believers who have served well will live richly rewarded in peace and rest with the Holy and Almighty God and Our Blessed Father, Ablo. Sobeit, Ablo, Sobeit."

D'Fro turned to T'Roo and said, "I don't believe it. You look as bad as I feel. Seems I am not the only one who barely slept at all last night. All I could think about was each and every word I said last night, questioning whether they heard what I was saying or if I was accidentally making the world's worst first impression."

"I know the feeling. I didn't sleep last night either. All I could think about was what if I forget to climb down the ladder and just jump off the bed as I have always done at home, for as long as I can remember? And if I do, how much will that hurt?" T'Roo said.

D'Fro laughed. "That is no surprise. I can imagine how that could happen. These beds are so different. I just know it will take time for me to get used to sleeping this high above the ground. It looks like a shower will do us both some good, so we have to take one, as public as they are. With most of our families being able to afford houses with multiple bathrooms, you would think they would design these dorm rooms with private bathrooms as well, but no. Oh, well, we had better get going. Busy day, busy day," D'Fro said as she hurried to gather up all her shower supplies, along with her nerve.

"How many things do you need in the shower?" T'Roo asked.

"Almost everything! Soap to cleanse my body, moisturizer to keep that soap from drying out my skin, shampoo and conditioner and curling iron. In short, the barest of necessities for keeping up appearances. After all, do not forget, it is all about looking your best while doing your best," D'Fro answered.

"Yes, indeed," a dazed and confused T'Roo softly said. She gazed upon her own shower supplies, consisting solely of a bar of soap. To change the subject, she added, "At least we only pass one doorway on the way to the showers. I guess that is the price we pay for living among the closest to the patios. Then again, perhaps we should count this as the blessing of proper planning. After all, they did plan this floor well enough so that no one walks all that far to the restrooms and showers.

"Re-examine the floor plan again. Is this really the best floor plan that the builders could have come up with? After all, by simply adding a private shower and restroom to each room, would that not make each room that much better, even if it results in a few fewer rooms," D'Fro argued.

"As much as I agree with you, you also forget about this college's history, of which my oldest sister reminded me when she found out I was about to start college. It's a historical fact that this dorm building was built before indoor plumbing of any kind had even been imagined, let alone invented," T'Roo said.

"Well, I don't care about this dorm's history. It should have been remodeled to accommodate showers and restrooms in every room," D'Fro persisted.

"Or you could be grateful that we were born after indoor plumbing. After all, as inconvenient as it is to walk into one center restroom to relieve ourselves and to wash our hands and brush our teeth and to walk across the hall to shower, imagine how much worse it would have been to have to step outside to shower and to relieve ourselves, especially in the winter. No doubt, those winter showers must have been cut short, and they must have done some very fast running in and out," T'Roo said.

"I don't care how much worse the early students of this college had it. At least those early students were too busy freezing or trying not to freeze to have time to worry about who was watching them and what other early students were thinking about as they were watching them. Those early students were too busy keeping themselves from freezing to death to worry how many of the other students were probably … probably … how do I say it?" D'Fro said, becoming too frustrated to continue.

"You mean you are afraid homosexuals may be watching you, or think that we are homosexual or have homosexual tenancies. Thank you for reminding me. I was hoping for one less thing to worry about," T'Roo said.

"Well, you should be worried. We do need to guard our reputations at all times and at any cost. Once rumors get started, they cannot be stopped and some even continue well after graduation." D'Fro continued to complain until they started to overhear another conversation.

"V'To wait! On second thought, don't wait or may do wait or don't wait if you don't unless you mind waiting. Final thought, do wait, please," the young lady from across the hall said.

"Are you sure? Are you absolutely certain that we should be seen going into the shower room together?" V'To asked.

"Not when you say it like that. Maybe not then, but then again, I am not actually sure if I want to walk into there all by myself. I think I need back up," her roommate explained.

"Greetings. My name is T'Roo, and this is my roommate, D'Fro. So, you two must be the ones who got the other far room," she nervously said, wearing only her sleepwear and house robe.

"Yes, we are. This person is my roommate, V'To, and my name is K'Lo. We were just discussing whether it would be wiser for all appearances' sake to enter the showers together or separately. After all, going in with backup does have a certain appeal. Yet, if it is viewed as something else, it might invite some of the nastiest gossips," she explained in a low whisper, watching to see whether anyone else was listening.

"Yes, I understand, but I do like the idea of going in with backup. If we all go in together, we can get through this idea of public showers and being undressed in front of everybody," D'Fro agreed.

"Sadly, there is a reason for the freshmen's dorms to be built like this. These were built long before indoor plumbing was even conceived of. According to my research, originally, this was the senior dorm, and originally there was only one lady per room. There were public outhouses, and how each student washed up was up to them," V'To explained.

"Wow! They had to step outside, even in the winter, way out there in the public, to relieve themselves, even when the temperatures dropped to sub-zero degrees. No wonder public showers did not bother them. After all, anything was better than having to step outside in the winter. Besides that, they were conditioned to have people see them at their worst," D'Fro exclaimed.

"They have since built the newer dorms for the upperclassmen. They built the newest dorms for the graduate students, who are getting their higher, even more affluent degrees. After all, why do you think D'Con is working as F'Ree's assistant?" V'To continued to explain.

"I haven't thought about that, and I likely never would have. So, I suppose you are going to enlighten us," T'Roo said.

"D'Con is no doubt a graduate student who is working here to supplement her education, since the more you volunteer your time, the more the government likes it," V'To explained. "Don't you know that we freshmen have yet to earn the privilege of private showers or restrooms? We are the lowest class of students here. We must work our way up the ladder."

"And how would you know all that?" T'Roo asked. "One thing I do know is that we had better hurry up and hit the showers while there is still some hot water and we still have time to make it to breakfast."

"Good point," V'To said. "Oh well, looks like we have no other choice. It is written in the *Holy Book of Ablo* that cleanliness is the first step to holiness. It looks like we all have to learn how to take public showers," D'Fro said. The others nodded in agreement. They started toward the showers. V'To said, "These public showers should be simple. My family has been attending Saint I'Bar College since the day it was built. In addition to that, as I said before, I did my research at Saint I'Bar College. Reading the various histories is my favorite hobby." As she continued to talk, her companions enjoyed the blissful distraction it provided. "Essentially, it can be quite easy if you remember to fix your gaze on the ceiling. Then, no one can accuse you being any kind of pervert. That is what I plan to do, as I hope and pray to Our Holy God and Blessed Father, Ablo, that no one is there to watch me," V'To said.

T'Roo said as they enter the shower area, "I remember my sisters telling me about them and how that is something that one simply must adjust to. Neither of them told me how or why, but they did agree that if one does have a conversation with someone else while in the shower room to keep one's mind and eyes focused on their noses and nothing lower than that. That was their way of surviving this lack of privacy. The college uses it as motivation to graduate to the next level that much quicker."

T'Roo took off her robe and nightwear as quickly as possible. She showered up and ran out as quickly and as carefully as she could, successfully keeping her eyes on the floor, which also served to keep her from slipping and falling. T'Roo, having barely dried herself off and wiggled her cold, wet body back into her nightwear and house robe, soon made it back to her dorm room, most grateful that she kept her shower short. She chose not to wait for D'Fro, since she did not want to know how long it took to go through her shower routine. There she got dressed in her closet and left, wearing one of her more casual pantsuits for breakfast, as D'Fro was coming back from the showers. T'Roo was among the earliest freshmen students to walk over to the dining hall. There they waited for others before beginning the first morning prayers as the first round of breakfast was served. As usual, they commenced with opening prayer and move on to the meal prayer before eating. After they finished eating, they waited to be handed their schedules, which were handed out by floor. "Floor number and room number?" D'Con asked as she sat at the tableful of papers and folders.

"Fourth floor, room seven," T'Roo answered.

As she pulled out the folder in room seven, D'Con said, "Show me one of your hands, and I will see if your prints match with one of the students assigned to the room." Upon studying her hand, she said, "According to photo and prints, you are indeed T'Roo. You will find your photo and your fingerprint card in your folder. Keep them on you, and be prepared to show them when you least expect it. That way, we can keep you safe from impersonators. You will find that if you invest in a small binder, you can carry them safely throughout your first year." She handed T'Roo her folder, which primarily held her class schedule.

As T'Roo walked away, she read her schedule. Her first class was in just over a half-hour. Language, with Professor O'Mar Chvo.

"Don't lose the last page. It is just as important as the other pages. That map should keep you from getting lost," D'Con warned her as T'Roo ambled away.

As T'Roo walked back to her dorm, she spied K'Ree. "K'Ree, it is indeed nice to see you this morning. How are you doing?" T'Roo said.

"Well, since my flowers and trees are doing excellent this blessed morning, how can I feel anything but fine? And yourself?" K'Ree responded.

"Fine, I guess. Classes are only just about to begin, so I am excited and nervous," T'Roo said.

"Just remember to focus that nervous energy on your studies and you will do more than just fine. You will excel. Good day, Miss T'Roo. Take care. I have other gardens calling me, so I must go."

The Language Arts Building was an eight-story red-stone building that stood head and shoulders above most other buildings, such as the merely two-story Student Affairs Building, which housed the bookstore, the four-story Mathematics Building, and even the five-story History Building and the seven-story Science Building. However, head and shoulders above them all was the thirteen-story Theological Studies Building.

There, T'Roo entered the Language Arts Building, pushing her empty bag behind her. She was self-conscious and fearful that she looked all too silly. As she climbed her way to the top floor, her mind wandered back to, oldest sister T'Fra saying, "You are about to enter college now. That littlest-sister shyness has got to end. It is not cute anymore." Another older sister, T'Lee, had said, "You are in college. Now is the time to make as many friends as you can, and with any luck and a wing and a prayer, Ablo will bless you with a good husband from one of them." After climbing all the way to the top floor, she took a deep breath, bolstering her determination to do as her sisters had told her to do as she walked into the classroom.

"Hey, T'Roo! This desk is open. Come on over and sit here before someone else does," D'Fro yelled out, pointing at the desk right next to her. "Thank you so very much for leaving our room to myself so that I could get dressed in private."

"Thanks for saving me a seat, and you're welcome." T'Roo's voice faded away as she forced a smile, quietly and meekly sitting down.

"Oh, I am ever so glad to see you. You are the one and only person whom I know in this room. As you can see, everyone already knows everyone else. By the way, please tell me that you know someone other than me whom you can introduce me to. Please, tell me," D'Fro quietly pleaded.

"I am sorry, but I can't. You are the only person that I know here too. Yes, everyone else in here is a stranger to me too," T'Roo explained as she felt her fear renewed.

The door slammed shut.

"Well, now that I have everyone's attention, let me introduce myself. I am Professor O'Mar Chvo, whom everyone missed at the Freshmen Dinner, the very same whose absence was no doubt the subject of much speculation. First, let me sort the non-fiction from the fiction. I was not there because I am not here to be impressed by anyone. As you can plainly see, I do indeed wear the skirt in the family. Each person here must earn my respect as sure as each person must earn their own grades. No doubt, there many professors here who enjoy and even revel in politics, but I am first and foremost a professor of language and literature, not a politician. Second, let us get straight to the business of who sits where."

The elder statesman reached for a piece of paper. As he read off names, he pointed to desks until each desk had a person assigned to it. "Now that each person is sitting in their proper seat, the next order of business is to hand out the class synopsis. This handout, which I expect everyone to read, also includes a list of additional supplies. The final order of business is textbooks, which your parents have already paid for, since it was included in the price of your tuition. Before you leave, there will be essays, and term papers will be expected of you. The subject matter will cover forms of literature spoken and written not only here in West Shire but also the other shires of Norhem. All dialects of Norhem are taught here, since you may be required to do missionary work or business in one or more of the other shires. May Our Holy God and Blessed Father, Ablo, speed you on your way. Do enjoy today's shortened class period, for it will be the only one you will ever have, barring any natural or national disasters. Don't forget that the backup generator for this building works very well and is indeed well guarded, so don't expect that just because your dorm room has lost power the class will be canceled. Come to class anyway. There will be a note on the door. The best rule to follow is *better safe than sorry*. Good day, students."

Leaving a half-hour early from her Language class, T'Roo decided to go straight to the Mathematics Building, which was in the opposite direction of the Student Affairs Building. Once again, her class was on the top floor. She began to realize that all her classes would be on the top floor, the price of being a freshman yet again. As she walked, she kept an eye out for the gardener, K'Ree, whom she was hoping to see yet again. She wondered if she was making a mistake by not going straight to the bookstore. However, to turn around and go back now might take even longer, which would be an even worse mistake. After all, she was now committed to arriving at Math class early, and for now, she was grateful that her bag had both extending straps and the option for wheels. Arriving on the fourth floor early, T'Roo was happy to see the small student lounge area very close to her classroom. It was a beautiful but dark wood-paneled room, with nearly as many wall lights as her dorm room hallway, but here there was an occasional window along with the usual portraits of the God Ablo, ones of him blessing his Saint I'Bar and other pictures of him blessing the Prime Minister E'Li Shro. There among the many chairs she sat and studied the handout she had received from her previous class, among the list of material needed for the class. She pondered, *It is a good thing that so many of these chairs have desk lamps next to them. When I have to catch up on my reading, using them will be the only way that I can do so. After all, I have a feeling I may turn one on just to read these lists. I wonder, how long will I be the only one here? I should have gone to the bookstore instead of coming straight here. Oh well, it is too late to worry about it now. After all, if I do leave, just to get stuck in a long line, I will probably get back here late for class, and then no one will believe that I was the first one here. Well, I do see a thing or two that I don't have and will soon need, but between T'Fra and T'Lee, they gave me excellent advice on what to get for college. It looks like I should indeed be thankful for being the youngest.*

T'Roo heard the sound of a door open and close. Needing something to do, she investigated it. To her delight, she discovered that other students had begun arriving to class.

"Greetings, I am—" T'Roo started to say to the young man sitting next to her, but he just turned away and started talking with other students.

The class's attention was called to the chalkboard, where they saw a woman, rather young for a college professor, with long blue hair smartly tied back, writing on the board. She said, "Welcome, freshmen and future mathematicians. This is College Algebra 1, and I am Professor T'Bii Tro. This young man here is my intern, O'Pam," she stated as she pointed him out to her class, even though he visibly appeared to be at least three to five years older than the students. After doing so, she continued, "For now, it is my challenge to teach your young minds how to think like college students, whether or not you pursue a career in mathematics." She paused as she picked up an object. "This is a slide rule. By the Grace of Ablo, I will be teaching you how to use it. You will need one if you do not have one already. After all, the way to learn how to use it is by using it. For now, I will permit this seating arrangement. If you want to sit somewhere else, you have five seconds to sit there. Otherwise, when I hand out the seating chart, I expect you to write your name and dorm room with your own pen in the appropriate square. Having your own supplies is a must for this class. Also, take note, this will be the one and only time that pens will be allowed in class. Otherwise, it is expected that you do your work in pencil, since mistakes are a given in mathematics regardless of branch." With that, she handed out the seating chart.

"How do we know if we are filling in the correct square?" a male student called out, causing many students to snicker.

Professor T'Bii walked up to him. "Young man, since this rectangle is my desk, then this first square must be your desk. No laughing. It is better to verify than to make a mistake, which would force this class to start all over with the seating chart." She pointed them out on the sitting chart as she continued, "While we are doing that, we also have other things to get done before I give you your first homework assignment. Now, as far as the books go, I will be handing out the textbook, but each one of you is responsible for getting your own workbook, which is listed on this handout. Be forewarned, getting supplied is the easy part of the class. Therefore, do not make it any harder than it has to be. After all, to most of you, if not all of you, algebra is all too new, even though you have been applying many of its principles without really thinking about it."

O'Pam pushed the cart of books up and down the rows and continued to hand out the textbooks.

"What do you mean that there will be homework? Who would give homework out on the first day?" a female student called out.

"I would, and I know many other instructors who will do likewise. Incidentally, your first homework assignment is to read the course synopsis, cover your books, buy the supplies as needed, and, above all, read the introduction at the beginning of the textbook. My seating chart, who has it? Pass it to me. I'll read the names. You raise your hand." As she read off each name, each person raised their hand, and so she continued, "Good. Everyone had better be sitting where they wanted to sit and with whom they wanted to sit. Otherwise, be prepared to learn to like the person you are sitting with, since I do not plan on changing the seating chart anytime soon. All praises are unto Our Holy God and Blessed Father, Ablo. Class, we are off to a good start. Class dismissed. By the way, this will be the one and only day that class gets discharged early. From now on, expect to stay seated until the bell finishes ringing and not a second earlier." Professor T'Bii sat down at her desk.

Having left the Mathematics Building, T'Roo finally saw the gardener, K'Ree. "Greetings, K'Ree, and good afternoon—or near afternoon, I should say. I am ever so happy to see you once again. You are such a breath of fresh air, a fresh point of view. I almost gave up hope that I would see you again. This first day of classes is becoming exhausting. I have never climbed so many stairs in my life, and I have only been to two classes so far. But the question should be, how are you and the flowers doing this blessed day?"

"We are fine. Thank you for asking. Relax and take a deep breath. Remember, this is only your first day of classes. After a few weeks or so, this walk will become easier and easier—at least compared to the homework. And as far as the homework goes, the only thing that anyone can demand from you is that you do your very best. No one can ask anything more than that," K'Ree explained.

"Yes, I do plan on doing my best, even if I do not do as well as both my older sisters did," T'Roo said.

"No, no! That is not what I am talking about. You just do the best you can. That is all anyone, including yourself, can ask of you. As long as you stay true to and with yourself, Our Holy and Blessed Father, Ablo, will surely bless you with success. I feel it in my bones," K'Ree reassured her. "By the way, from what I hear, the Freshmen Dinner went well. After all, there was no increase in campus security, uniformed or otherwise. I'll tell you a little secret, just between the two of us. The surest sign that the dinner was a complete disaster is when campus security suddenly multiplies. Also, do not forget, the security officers that you need to fear the most are the ones dressed as civilians." Seeing the fear in T'Roo's eyes, K'Ree lightheartedly added, "What am I talking about? The dinner was also supposed to be enjoyable. How did you enjoy yourself? You did enjoy yourself to some degree, I hope."

"I guess I enjoyed it well enough. After all, it went well enough not to stir up any trouble. Sounds like that was a good sign. Even though, between that dinner and my first two classes, the only three friends I can honestly say I have even come close to making are you, my roommate, D'Fro, and D'Li," T'Roo said with a heavy sigh.

"Oh, relax, T'Roo. Today is only Orientation Day. I believe you should have at least three more classes left, along with lunch and supper, so you shall have that many more chances to meet new people and make friends. Just remember, they are as nervous about meeting you as you are about meeting them. Now, take care, be confident, and go with Our Holy God and Blessed Father, Ablo. I am sorry, but I must excuse myself, as I have other gardens that need tending. Farewell and fare thee well," K'Ree said as she departed.

How did she know my class schedule so well? One would think that she knows my schedule better than I know it. However, the question to drop off these textbooks or not? Which would be the easiest thing to do, lighten the load or extend the distances walked. "Oh, how I miss those grade schools, where all you had to do was listen to what the teachers told you to do," T'Roo mumbled to herself as she was left just standing there in confusion and amazement. As she studied her schedule and the campus map once again, she finally decided to drop off these textbooks in her dorm room. There, she walked through the silent hallway, all by herself. She wondered if she had made the right decision, since apparently she was the only one who had made it. As she was turning her key, she heard a voice.

"Greetings, but don't you have more classes to go to." It was F'Ree, who was suddenly behind her.

"Yes, but I thought it would be easier to get to the other classes and lunch with a lighter load," T'Roo explained.

"Yes, I understand that. So let us both make certain that we keep to our appropriate schedules. It would do neither of us any service to be late," F'Ree said as she was dashing down the hall.

"Yes, indeed and good day," T'Roo said. She pondered, *I could have … I would have sworn that I was alone in this hallway, but yet there she was. How did I miss her?*

Afterward, T'Roo went straight to the campus bookstore, which was uneventful but time-consuming, because, to her disappointment, she suddenly found herself with everyone else, who were still picking up supplies. She would need to take a fast lunch, since she barely had time for the meal blessing let alone eating. Thus, instead of the main dining hall, she was left to eat by her lonesome in the outer room. There she was left to whisper the prayer by herself. She pondered, *I wonder, if I whisper it soft enough, will anyone notice or even care if I cut it short? I do hope Our Holy God and Blessed Father Ablo will forgive me, especially if I swear by all that I hold holy never, ever to cut any of my prayers to him short, ever again.* As there is also a reading section at the bookstore, many students have their heads buried into a book there, leaving T'Roo to feel very much alone in a crowd.

T'Roo's next class was Physical Education. Upon arriving at the female locker room, she saw signs pointing toward the gymnasium, which she and the others followed.

A mature woman was speaking through a loudspeaker. "Just take a seat on the benches. We have much to cover today. As soon as everyone is present, we can get started. Good, Thank Ablo, it looks like everyone is here. Good. Well, ladies, I am T'Alo Bo. I am the physical fitness professor. These are my interns, with whom you will become familiar as the classes go along, so you do not need to know their names yet. The first orders of business is gym uniforms and locker assignments, including locks, both of which were included in your price of tuition. As I call your name and dorm room, come down and pick up your bag from my intern, who will also confirm your correct size. I then expect you all to return to your seats. Tomorrow, those who need new clothes will report to my office, and you will trade in the clothes you have for proper-fitting ones. Is that understood?" Professor T'Alo began reading off names and numbers, including T'Roo's. "Good, everyone is present—"

Professor T'Alo started before getting a tap on the shoulder.

"Professor, what should I do? My shoes and socks are the wrong sizes," a student asked.

"What did I just finish saying, young lady?" Professor T'Alo growled.

"Ahem. To go to your office, where I can trade them in for the proper sizes, but what if you don't have my size?" she timidly questioned.

"Don't worry about that. Wrong sizes rarely happen. However, on the very rare occasion that it does, all I have to do is order the right size, and the new physical education clothes usually, if not always, come the next day. So don't worry about it." Professor V'Alo added, "By the way, there will be no stuttering in this class. If you have something to say, just say it or don't say it. This in-between nonsense is a waste of time. This applies to everyone. Young lady, this will be taken care of before your first class. This goes for everyone else who got the wrong size for any of their gym clothes. Now, does everyone understand?"

"Yes, Professor V'Alo Bo," the class said in unison.

"Now that we finally have that business done with, we might even understand each other. As you can see, there are tables behind me. As I call up each row of benches, each student will sign up for various gym classes throughout this semester. The last row does not panic. Each class is offered at various times throughout this semester. If you cannot take that class first or second, then surely the option of third of forth will be open. There are indeed plenty of classes. The classes include individual sports such as archery, swimming, and gymnastics, along with team sports such as kickball, relay racing, and others. Please remember, team sports are open to larger classes, which is why they are encouraged. As soon as you are signed up for your classes, you may leave. So, let us get started. Row one."

T'Roo was left to wonder on her way to her next class, Archaean History, *Should I have been grateful that I was sitting in the first row? After all, it was thanks to that fact that I got to take the gym classes that I wanted to take. Now, the only question is, did I choose my gym classes wisely, or did I make a big, huge terrible mistake picking football first? Oh, how I miss grade school. Back then, we were told what the activity for that gym class was going to be for that day, and we blissfully did not have to decide anything.*

All too soon, the Achaean History class began, with each student getting assigned a desk to sit at. This professor, Professor I'Var Fro, also began the usual lecture on what the class would be about and what was expected of them, followed by the handing out of their history books. As mental exhaustion began to set in from hearing basically the same set of instructions yet again, T'Roo overheard two students complain that they had set through this exact same lecture at each and every class so far. T'Roo wished she had the nerve to jump in and agree with them, but since she did not know either of the two students who were whispering, she thought it best not to intrude. That might only serve to get them caught talking in class. If only she had the nerve, she would have added that this was turning into the longest day of her life thus far. But at that point, she could just hear the professor yelling at them all, and then they would really have a good reason to hate her.

T'Roo walked over to the Science Building and toward her classroom. She pondered, *Oh, great, yet another class on the top floor. Well, at least this is my final official class of the day. It'll be the last time today I need to sit through the typical seating assignments and the same old speech of what this class will be about, and this is what you are expected to learn, and these are the additional supplies that only our bookstore carries, so everyone must buy them here and so on.* She sat and waited for the final tardy bell to ring so the professor could begin the class.

"Greetings and congratulations. Upon the end of this class, we all will be able to state that we have survived our first day of college. I am Professor O'Well Thro, and this class is Freshman Science, where I get to introduce you to all the sciences by which Our Holy God and Blessed Father, Ablo, has sanctified us all, by bestowing us with the capacity to talk and to think, and especially the capacity to make life better. Without further ado, yes, the seating assignment comes first, so let us get started: E'Bar Bo," he called out, pointing to a desk. "I'Ram Fro, T'Roo Mo, D'Lir Wo, I'Mar Bro …"

He continued to assign seats until each of the thirty-four students was sitting at their own assigned desk.

"Professor, one question, sir," D'Lir said.

"Just one, young lady?"

"Well, my first question of the day. Since our textbooks are so thick, can we assume that we won't be needing workbooks, as we do for other classes?"

"I hate to break it to everyone, especially to Miss D'Lir here, but even though your Freshmen Science is most likely the thickest book you will have this year, yes, you will still need to invest in workbooks. In fact, each science, from Physics to Chemistry and others, will have its own workbook to hand in. That way, there will be more to your grade than just exams and quizzes. After all, as I was saying before, this is your introduction to the sciences. These are the sciences that Our Holy God and Blessed Father, Ablo, has blessed us with, and thanks to the saints and prophets, through whom she has spoken, we have the valued instruction that the sciences should not be taught until well after one's faith has been established, lest it should cause confusion within the fledgling mind. In fact, the first science we shall learn about will be Astronomy. Thanks to the inventiveness of a young man whose family is too poor to afford the tuition here, prompting him to seek a scholarship, tomorrow's class will be pushed back well into the evening. Instead of gathering in this classroom and doing the usual reading about the stars, we will be gathered on the roof and perhaps even look at the stars up close, through this spyglass that this young man has invented. We will see if he has indeed earned a scholarship here, and who knows what we may discover about the stars? All thanks to Our Holy God and Blessed Father, Ablo, for his inspiration. Scientists have been inspired to create electricity to light the night so that we may read Our Holy God and Blessed Father, Ablo's, written word throughout the day and throughout the night. So tonight, I expect you to have your *Introduction to the Sciences* book, but instead of reporting to class at this time, go to sleep or do whatever you need to do to be up and alert tomorrow night, when the class will be held on the roof. That is all I have. Class is dismissed. Go in peace. Thanks be to Our Holy God and Blessed Father, Ablo."

After supper, on the way to practice, she read various signs about ensembles to try out for, so she approached the front desk and asked the receptionist, "I see that there are tryouts for various ensembles. I would like to try out for one. Which one has an opening for a Norhemian lyre player?"

"Good question. Let me check my records. I know the one that I am in, a woodwind ensemble, is looking for a new fife player. Oh, here we go. There is a string ensemble whose lead Norhemian lyre player just graduated, which means that they are looking for a new backup Norhemian lyre player. That is, unless you can take the lead away from her. Either way, they are taking tryouts, but the bad news is you will be the third person trying out for that chair. The question is, do you still want to try out for that chair?" the receptionist asked. "Are you really sure that you are ready to commit to an ensemble? After all, they are required to try out for every church service they perform in and to try out for every performance they play in. Are you sure you are ready for that—that is, if you get the chair?"

"Yes, I am. Please point me to where the tryout is."

T'Roo walked in to hear the alto lyre player scolding, "Now listen here, this national anthem of ours is a fundamentally easy tune, especially since we all have been playing it ever since we each started to play our instruments. I play the lead alto lyre, which means I play the lead and you play one of the Norhemian lyres that accompany me, along with another alto lyre and bass lyre. You have got to learn to follow me. You are not following."

"Excuse me, but I am a good follower. Could you please try me?" T'Roo asked.

"All right. The chair is open and may become yours. Let us listen and see what you have got." The Norhemian lyre player spoke as if to challenge T'Roo, who did her best to keep up.

"Yes, the chair is yours," said the alto lyre player along with the rest of the ensemble.

CHAPTER 5

WELCOME TO FOOTBALL

T'Roo started her day with communal morning showers in the company of her roommate. This was slowly becoming as routine as morning prayers and power outages, along with keeping an eye open for the gardener, K'Ree, between classes and meals. During Language class, Professor O'Mar Chvo interrupted his lecture to ask, "T'Roo, our founding fathers agreed to designate one dialect for business. Why was that important?"

"Excuse me, Professor. Why was what important?" T'Roo asked as she turned her attention to the professor.

"You would know the answer if you were paying attention, young lady. Now T'He, would you care to enlighten Miss T'Roo and the rest of the class as to why that would be so? That is, unless Miss T'Roo would rather enlighten us all to what could be more important than this class," Professor O'Mar scolded. T'Roo was struck silent, with the feeling that her heart had just sunk into her stomach. The eyes of all her classmates seemed to be on her, along with the feeling of nausea that comes with it. The professor continued by asking another student that same question. Then, to T'Roo's relief, the chimes rang, signaling the end of class and what T'Roo thought was her ordeal. That was, until Professor O'Mar asked, "T'Roo, what is today's homework assignment?"

"Read chapter one, the early authors and playwrights of West Shire. Since everyone here was born and raised in West Shire, everyone should be familiar with the dialect, so there will be no problems reading the assignment or answering any of the review questions thoroughly," T'Roo repeated.

"Congratulations. So, young lady, you really can pay attention after all. Let this be a lesson, students. You cannot move ahead into the future without a thorough understanding of where we have been. After all, each and every one of these authors and playwrights wrote for the glory of Our Holy God and Blessed Father, Ablo. Good day, students, and May Our Holy God and Blessed Father, Ablo, continue to be with you throughout this day."

Fortunately, T'Roo's Algebra class commenced with only the usual ten- to fifteen-minute delay to get the lights back on and even more homework.

T'Roo's mind wandered yet again as she changed out of her street clothes and into her gym clothes. She had chosen football as her Physical Education as she had overheard various conversations that the class had been selected was fun. However, many of her classmates classmates elected it to make it to the college's football team, even though the women's teams played only intramural games, as opposed to the men's football team. She reported to the freshmen's football field, located in one of the sub-basements. The Physical Education Professor T'Alo Bo called, "Students, gather around and take a seat on the floor. Quickly and quietly. The sooner I can explain the rules, the sooner you can get kick the balls around. There will be a review of the rules of the game, since I do not have referees to back me up here. I hope everyone is aware that the game starts when the baller rolls the ball down to the first kicker, who then kicks the ball with their foot into play. Hence the name of the game, football. I need you all to have a thoroughly clear understanding of the rules so there will be no questioning or second-guessing of my calls. Is that clear?"

"Yes, Professor T'Alo Bo!" the football class said.

"Say what? I did not hear you. Do you understand or not that after we review the rules of the game, you will have a thorough understanding of these rules so that you will not argue nor debate my play calling?" Professor T'Alo persisted.

"Yes, Professor, we understand," the class shouted even louder than before.

"Good. Then let us get started. There won't be time to have a game, but we should get some practice in kicking, rolling, and even catching and throwing the ball so that no one has any excuses once the games begin. Now follow me." Professor T'Alo walked over to the chalkboard stationed against the outfield wall. She continued, "Class, sit down and make yourselves as comfortable as you can on the floor."

"Yes, Professor," the class replied.

"First things first, class," Professor T'Alo said. She picked up a ball and continued, "This is the ball we will be using in class. Note that it is thirteen inches in diameter. It is made out of a softer rubber, which is far softer than the leather that the men play with, but if it hits you, it will still sting. The bounciness of the ball is why paying attention in class is so very important, because it can easily bounce right into your face, which is also why I do not deduct points for inattentiveness. I don't have to. The opposing team and the ball will do that for me. Now, take it and pass it around, and note that it has quite a bounce to it. Once the game starts, the offensive team can use it to their favor, which is something I do not recommend to the defensive team, since it only slows down the ball."

"What do you mean we can 'use the bounce' in our favor?" one of the students asked.

"You are getting ahead of me, but I am glad that you want to know. When you walk over to home base—which you cannot miss, since it is the only position that has two lines parallel to it, both lines each three feet away from the plate—the baller must roll the ball between those two lines for the kicker to be held responsible for kicking the ball. Should the baller fail to do so, it is counted as a baller's error. After the second baller's fault, the kicker is given first position, or first post, for short. Now, back to your question. Since this ball bounces so effortlessly, kicking it high to the outfield wall keeps it in play yet out of the fielders' hands, and many have found that doing so is an excellent way to score. It is impossible to kick it outside the park the same way that men's football can, but that is the reward the men get for playing the game outside in all the elements. If anyone has ever watched a men's game of football, then you already know that the one and only time a game gets called for weather is if there is a thunderstorm. Other than that, they play in the rain, in a heatwave, or even during the coldest of days—even if it is snowing. Is everyone still with me?"

"Yes, Professor," the class responded.

"Excellent, we covered baller's errors. Now it is time for the kicker's error. That is when the ball is rolled down between the two parallel lines but the kicker fails to put it in play. Should a kicker do that four times, that becomes an out. There are four outs per period. In women's football, especially here in physical education class, games are called at fifteen minutes before class ends so no one has an excuse not to shower up before their next class. Speaking of outs, there are other ways that outs occur. Does anyone know?"

"When a player catches the ball in flight," one student said.

"Yes, that is close. You forgot to add without bouncing anywhere, but yes, that is good and the other. Anyone?" Professor T'Alo said, looking around. "The other way that an out happens is when a fielder throws the ball to the position person just before the runner gets there. I believe that covers all the rules, so that gives us some time. We have a basket full of balls here. Everyone spread out and just kick the ball against the wall. Hopefully, you can catch it. That way, you not only get the feeling of kicking but catching too." The professor walked around observing the players kicking the ball against the wall and catching it with various degrees of success. She advised one person to kick the ball with the side of her foot so she could get more control and more power behind the kick. She advised the others to keep their hands up, as the last thing that they wanted was for the ball to hit them in the face. Soon, class ended.

Thank Ablo that History was nicely uneventful, just a nice boring lecture that was straight out of the book. I do believe that I underlined only the most important parts, or at least I hope and pray that I did. On her way to the dining hall for supper, she pondered, *I wonder where K'Ree is. These gardens are so empty and lonely without her. Either I am constantly missing her or, I wonder, could this be her day off?*

After supper, she did her homework and took a short nap so she could be well rested for that evening's Science class.

CHAPTER 6
PROFESSOR O'WELL'S SCIENCE CLASS

That evening, T'Roo was about to walk into the Science Building when a voice stopped her.

"Hold it, young lady," the watchman said. "At the risk of proving how old I am, you do not look like you are anywhere near old enough to be doing your postgraduate work. It is a well-known fact that only postgraduate study classes are scheduled at night—in fact, they occur only at night—which begs the question: What are you doing out here at this late hour?" he questioned her.

"Yes, sir, that is true, and I know that undergraduate classes, and especially all freshmen classes, are held during the day. However, our freshman science class is about to do a special astronomy project that we can only do at night, since that is the only time the stars can be seen," T'Roo explained.

Suddenly, another watchman stepped forward. "Oh, yes, this young lady is telling the truth. Professor O'Well Thro told some of the other watchmen and me all about the project that his freshmen science class will be testing out tonight. I was just coming to tell you all about it. I am sorry. I wasn't expecting the students to start coming this early. The professor did ask if we would remind his students to go straight to the classroom and to do so as quickly and quietly as possible. After all, the whole point of scheduling the postgraduate studies at night is so that the postgraduate students can work with the least amount of disturbances possible, since even the slightest noise can become very loud when there are many voices. If all else fails, we should remind his students that this was how Norhem went from burning trees for electricity to burning methane gas for electricity. That was after the forests were too far spent to be useful."

"Yes, sir, I understand your point perfectly. Sir, I promise I will do everything that I can to make sure the postgraduate students do not even suspect that we are here," T'Roo reassured the watchman. She quietly walked past him and up the stairs to her classroom. As T'Roo entered the classroom, upon seeing the various other students, she asked, "Hold it. How did you make it past the night watchman? When I got to the door, I was questioned."

"Which entrance did you take?" I'Mar asked.

"The north entrance, as usual."

"See, that was your problem. I took the south entrance, where that watchman was already expecting us, so I didn't have any problems, only a lecture on walking softly and quietly," I'Mar responded

E'Bar added, "Or you could have done what I did. I returned here with my supper in my book bag instead of books. I ate my meal and took my nap here, until I'Mar over there woke me up. It wasn't the most comfortable nap I ever took, but at least I didn't have to deal with any night watchmen. Speaking of the nap that I didn't take, could anyone else imagine how useful it would be to see them before they saw us, or at least know that we were being watched?"

"Yes, we were just speculating on how the spyglass would be useful for our defense against So'hem. Would you care to speculate with us, at least until the professor arrives?" I'Mar asked.

"Isn't that a bit presumptuous? After all, we do not know how or if that thing works yet," D'Lir said as she walked through the door, with several other students following.

Moments later, Professor O'Well walked in. Even more students walked in along with him as he took a mental headcount. "Well, it looks like everyone is here, but I will double-check to give any stragglers time to arrive. That way we'll know how many won't be here. After all, this is not mandatory, only extra credit." After reading the class roll, he found out that out of thirty-four students, twenty-seven had arrived at the classroom. They would then proceed to the hallway that led them to the rope ladder that workers use to maintain the roof. Professor O'Well was the first look through the spyglass as he explained, "Permit me to demonstrate. I will make sure to keep this short so that you, my students, will have more time to use the device. Right now, I look up to see what appears to be the emptiness of space, by holding the spyglass up to my eye and adjusting the lenses thusly. Remember to experiment. If the image is getting foggier and foggier, that means that you are turning the knob in the wrong direction and you need to reverse your direction. Instead of empty space, I can now see them. There are rocks there. If I further adjust it, I can bring one rock into total focus. Any questions?"

The first student to gaze through the spyglass was E'Bar, who, in his state of shock, asked, "Professor O'Well, it appears that the sun also shines on this side of those rocks?"

"Yes, so do those rocks go around Archadea the same way that the sun and moons do?" a student asked.

E'Bar replied, "My older sister is an art major. One thing that I remember about her and her pictures is how light works on the canvas. I know about Archadea being the center, but the sunlight is on the wrong side of those rocks for that. I cannot explain this. After all, I know and trust the teaching of the *Holy Book of Ablo*, which openly states that our world, Archadea, is at the center of the universe. Therefore, everything in the universe goes around us, as ordained by Our Holy God and Blessed Father, Ablo, who spoke Archadea into existence at the moment of creation." In stunned disbelief, this student handed the spyglass to the student next to him.

"Are you sure about what you think you saw?" I'Mar questioned. "Let me take a look … Amazing … I can't believe it. Are my eyes deceiving me? It cannot be. The sun appears to be shining on that big yellow sphere with orange stripes. It has a very extensive ring around it and many rocks and several spheres circling it, as if the sun is the true center. But that cannot be. Speaking of moons, it would appear that Archadea is not the only world with moons. But why would Our Holy God and Blessed Father, Ablo, place moons … Hold it, if that sphere has moons that go around it, it might be another world. But how can there be other worlds when he only blessed Archadea with life? Yet, if Ablo did create other worlds, then Our Holy God and Blessed Father would have had no reason to place Archadea in the center; that would not have been fair to the other worlds, and one thing we know is that Our Holy God and Blessed Father is fair and just toward all his children," I'Mar concluded. "Professor, Professor," he called out. The professor just stood there in shocked disbelief as the students continued to pass the spyglass around.

"Yes, I can see that big yellow sphere with oh so many amazing stripes, but I don't see any ring. Hold it ... I see something happening. Right there, I see four yellow dots about to run into each other. Yes, they have, and now there is just one big red spot. Wow!" a student said.

"Wow! You were looking at something different than I was looking at. I wish I was looking at the sphere where the red dot was about to form instead of the one with the rings, no matter how many other spheres were going around it," I'Mar commented.

"Hold it, let me see. Which way were you pointing the spyglass when you saw the sphere with the ring around it, or better yet, the one with the brand-new red spot? Yes, I see it. It does appear as you describe. They both are so fascinating; both have so many spheres that seem to go around them. Even though they are traveling in completely different directions from each other, both have the sun shining on them. We must then conclude that they might be similar spheres, but they are, in fact, two different spheres," E'Bar said.

D'Lir commented next as she peered through the spyglass after having pointed it in both directions. "Amazing. I can hardly believe that I am actually seeing the exact same thing you saw, which means you really did see it or we both are being deceived by Jeho, which is highly unlikely, since Ablo would not allow that to happen here in her own country. Yes, it does appear that the sun is shining on those objects also, and those moonlike objects do appear to be casting shadows onto those spheres almost in the same manner that our main moon occasionally casts shade on us. I would therefore guess that would mean that the spheres are other worlds."

Next, it was T'Roo's turn. She looked out and began to describe what she saw. "That one star … No, it is another sphere. Hold it … there is another object, which appears to be a smaller sphere circling a much larger sphere. This must be what you were talking about seeing, another world with its own moon. Yet this one is different. This one has only one moon—or so it would appear—and this one is mostly blue, which reminds me of our very own rivers somehow. There are also smudges of green, which reminds me of our very own grass, which also has tans and browns. Believe it or not, the sun looks like it is shining on that one too, along with its moon. Yet we are Ablo's chosen people. Why would Our Holy God and Blessed Father create life there too?"

She passed the spyglass on to another student.

"Hold on! Let me see! Yes, I do see a blue sphere with a darker blue spot on it, but I only see very few white spots, and they're only around the darker blue spot. I do not see any tans or browns," the other student said.

"Well, no wonder. You have your spyglass pointed in a different direction," T'Roo responded.

"That must mean I am looking at a different blue sphere. By Our Holy God and Blessed Father, Ablo, how many blue spheres are there?" the same student exclaimed.

"That is another world with another ocean! After all, I can verify its moon, which may be the same size as our main moon. As I was about to say, I remember when I was little. My parents used to go to the beach because that was where my grandparents lived. I can still remember how the ocean looked, and how the waves would come ashore. The only discernable difference that I can see is their ground is lighter and tanner than our red land, but that hardly seems possible. Archadea is the one and only world that Our Holy God and Blessed Father, Ablo, blessed with life. That blue world may have an ocean, but how can it have intelligent life? Perhaps there is only fish life. But then why would Our Holy God and Blessed Father, Ablo, even put fish life on that world, since we cannot go fishing there? After all, Our Holy God and Blessed Father, Ablo, provides only for the needs of his sincere and devoted followers," the other student continued to say.

At last, Professor O'Well said in shocked disbelief, "Perhaps that extra-large star is indeed no star at all. Perhaps it does not really create its own light but merely reflects the light from our sun? It would appear there are other worlds with their own moon or moons and rings of rocks. Even more amazingly, the sun does appear to be shining on them all. I confess, I do not know what to say about all that we have seen this night. Let us all go back to our rooms and our beds and meditate on what Our Holy and Blessed Ablo has revealed to us. That is, if indeed it was Our Holy and Blessed God who has revealed all this to us. We must pray for wisdom to understand how these revelations, if true, must fit into her grand plan—somehow, some way. We can discuss it all in class tomorrow. The discussions will also include the possibility that this spyglass may be defective. Worst of all, it may have been cursed. I fear it may have been bewitched and all that we thought we were seeing was nothing more than Jeho's trickery, intended to make us question Our Holy

God and Blessed Father's sacred written word. If so, then we must all plead for Ablo's forgiveness and for her tender mercy to guide us all out of this darkness. May our Holy and Righteous God and Blessed Father, Ablo, guide us back into the light of his loving mercy. Sobeit, Our Holy God and Blessed Father, Ablo, Sobeit. Class dismissed. Besides, look at the way these clouds are starting to roll in. I would imagine that within the next hour or so, we will have at least some rain."

Later that same night, D'Con ordered, "Stop right there! No one, absolutely no one, asked for permission to be out this late. What were all of you doing out and about this far past your curfews? Somebody had better have an excellent, *a perfectly excellent*, explanation for this blatant breakage of the curfew."

"We had a special science class including a scientific experiment that could only happen after sunset," D'Lir explained.

The others nodded in agreement, while someone else blurted out, "If you don't believe us, why don't you ask Professor O'Well Thro?" They nodded in agreement at this also.

"Very well, I will check with the good professor in the morning, but be warned, if he does not verify your claim, you all will receive marks against you for breaking curfew. And if it happens again, you will face disciplinary action," D'Con warned the students before taking everyone's name.

CHAPTER 7
THE AFTERMATH

Later that evening, the rains did come. It left the drainage ditches full for hours but the sidewalks dry. This was a normal situation, just the start of another day, at least until physical education.

"Football Class, line up on this line," the professor instructed. After all the students were standing as directed, Professor T'Alo said, "Any questions about how the game of football is played before we get started?" As the class remained silent, the professor responded, "So, everyone has at least some understanding of how the game is played? Good. Let's play football. Where are my teams? Everyone, count off by two." After the class did so, she said, "All the 'ones' step forward to receive your black vests. You are now a team. I need one of you to step forward for the coin toss to decide who is on offense first. If your number was 'two,' you are the other team. Choose who will be your captain for the coin toss." All the twos, including T'Roo, looked at each other, until L'Ree stepped forward to be the captain. T'Alo pulled out a coin from her pocket and said, "Call it."

L'Ree spoke up first: "Heads!"

After the coin landed on the floor, Professor T'Alo declared, "Heads, indeed." She asked, "Offense or defense? And will your team be with or without black vests."

Without a moment of hesitation, L'Ree said, "Defense and without."

The team took to the field, with L'Ree claiming the spot of the baller for herself. T'Roo, being a somewhat less-than-eager player, claimed one of the three remaining outfield positions. The game started with L'Ree rolling the ball right down the middle and toward the kicker, who kicked the ball straight back at her. She caught it in flight and scored the first out. The second kicker kicked the ball right over the head of T'Roo, whose teammates yelled for her to hurry up and get the ball and throw it to one of the position players. She finally threw the ball to T'He, the second position player, even though the runner was safely on the third position, much to her teammates' chagrin. Fortunately for L'Ree and T'Roo's team, the next players all scored easy outs by kicking the ball straight in the air to various players, thus giving T'Roo a chance to redeem herself by scoring the final out and ending their turn at defense. Before anyone in the class knew it, the game and class were over, with the non-vested team winning seven to four. It was now time to hit the showers.

T'Roo meandered to her next class, Science. She read the same note on the door that the rest of her Science class had already read: "Professor O'Well's freshmen Science class is canceled due to his sudden illness."

"What? I don't remember the professor being sick last night," one student after another said in disbelief.

"No, I do not remember the professor complaining anything about his health," other students said.

"No, I don't remember the professor saying anything about not feeling well. He didn't look or act at all sick either," T'Roo said in agreement with the others as they all meandered away. Later that evening, after supper, T'Roo walked into the music department, signed in with the receptionist, and asked, "Is there a practice room open, or is anyone from the Beta String Ensemble here?"

"Yes on both counts. There is a practice room open, and the lead alto lyre player is looking for you—that is, if you are one of her players," the receptionist said.

"Yes, I am. I play the Norhemian lyre. Should I look for the lead alto lyre player, or will she find me?" T'Roo asked.

"Well, T'Roo, she, like everyone else here, has to see me before she leaves. So what I will do, since you will be going to practice room eleven, is let you get started with your individual practice session. When I do see her, I'll tell her you'll be there. I expect you'll be practicing for more than just a few minutes," the receptionist suggested.

"That would be a good idea. I usually practice for at least a half-hour if not longer," T'Roo said.

"Do you know where to find practice room eleven?" the receptionist asked.

"I believe I can find it on my own. After all, the doors are numbered, like the rest of the college," T'Roo responded.

"Yes, they are. So you should have no problems. Good luck," the receptionist said. T'Roo made her way to her practice room.

A few minutes into her practice, T'Roo heard a knock on the door and a voice that asked if she could come in.

"Yes, please enter," T'Roo said.

"Greetings. I hear you had questions about our practice schedule. Well, originally, it was individual practice as often as you want and ensemble practice if we happened to be here at the same time. But since there is that Grand Opening Ceremony at the new power plant, Saint I'Bar College was chosen to send our best string ensemble to perform the national anthem," the lead alto lyre player said.

"Hold it! Hold it! They want a string ensemble to play at the Grand Opening Ceremony of that big new power plant? The one they've been hyping up as the solution to all our current and future power outages? Isn't a Grand Opening like that the reason we have a concert band, to do major performances? I mean, aren't we small ensembles only for smaller events, like sporting events and dances?" T'Roo questioned.

"I know, it is unusual for an ensemble like ours to play this kind of major ceremony. All I know is that the powers that be have their reasons for downplaying the music. It is for them to know and for me not to question. After all, for all I know, they might have decided that having fewer musicians could allow for more honored guests," the lead alto lyre player answered. "Now, where was? Oh yes, as I will inform the others: if we are going to beat that Alpha String Ensemble for a change, we will need each person to do more individual practice sessions. The more often we are all here, the easier it will be to have group practices. Either way, we will all have to work that much harder so our very best is *the* very best. This is my senior year. I want this event on my resume more than anything on Archadea," the lead alto lyre player explained.

"Yes, I promise that I will practice more individually and with the ensemble and work my hardest to play better than I have ever played before—" T'Roo began to say.

"I don't want promises. I want *results*, from not only T'Roo but from the rest of you too, as well as from myself. Oh, if I can get this Grand Opening on my resume. This performance could make me the most sought-after alto lyre player, lead or backup, in all of Norhem. After all, as a senior, there is no next year for me. I don't think any of you understand—I mean, really understand—what it looks like on my college records that all my previous years at Saint I'Bar College, the Beta String Ensemble lost out to that Alpha String Ensemble, at more sporting events than I care to count. But not this time. This time, this big time, it will be Alpha String Ensemble's turn, along with all of Norhem, to stay home glued to the radio listening to me leading my Beta String Ensemble. I expect to make my last year my best year. Have I made myself clear?"

"Yes, you have. So I guess that there will be assigned practice sessions?" T'Roo asked.

"I don't know. I know I should, but I am also afraid that it may backfire on me. Let me put it this way. If people do not maintain more than a minimum number or duration of practice sessions, then I will assign practice hours, but if everyone keeps up on their own, I won't," the alto lyre player promised.

The day after that was the same, except for the Science class, where instead of the professor, T'Roo saw the chief of campus security, Officer K'Too Ko, who called for the students to assemble in front of their dorm mentor. The female students assembled around F'Ree, the dorm mentor of the female freshmen, and her assistant, D'Con Slo, while the male students were divided between both of the male dorm mentors and their assistants.

As F'Ree and D'Con both gathered several of the female students around them, the officer said, "Now hear this. This class is in some deep trouble—with not only the church but with the Norhem government. What I am about to tell you, you did not hear any of it from me. Is that understood?" she said in a very hushed whisper. When she heard no response from any around her, she repeated, "Is that understood?" At that, they slowly began to nod their heads, not so much in agreement but rather in shocked confusion.

"So, we imagined not only that Archadea is not, in fact, the center of the universe but also that our son is at the center of other worlds that go around it, just as Archadea does," T'Roo softly whispered.

"No, you probably did not, but the church and our government prefer to believe otherwise, and right now, they have all the power in the world you make and to break and to arrest anyone who dares tell them what they do not want to hear. This is especially true for freshmen students, who are the lowest of the low here in college, let alone in the great big world of Norhemian politics," Officer K'Too said in the same hushed whisper.

"What are we supposed to do, imagine that we did not learn anything from the experience of having looked through the spyglass? Shall we go on believing everything we are told to believe?" D'Lir asked.

"Yes, you are, at least for now. This culture is not ready to learn this harsh truth—or any other harsh truth. If and when you can gather enough people so that the church and the Norhemian government may be forced to listen to you instead of arrest you, then you can. But until that day comes, you will be speaking truth to the very same power that can and will crush you with only a light wave from their little pinkie finger," Officer K'Too said.

"So, is that how you will report this briefing went?" T'He asked.

"Not at all! After all, I do not have a death wish. I took the liberty of writing down exactly how this briefing went on my way here. The only thing that each of you needs to do is to remember this: Yes, you are loyal and faithful followers of Our Holy God and Blessed Father, Ablo, and his written words are holy and sacred and our source of stregth beyond question. Remember that Our Holy God and Blessed Father, Ablo, blessed Archadea with life so that he would not be alone, and he blessed Archadea with the beautiful night sky so that we can have beauty to inspire us. If anyone dares say anything else, it will be her own life she will be risking. Have I made myself clear?" They sat once again in dumb silence, so she repeated the question: "Have I made myself clear?"

"But is not the first rule that Ablo gave us to tell the truth, the whole truth, and only the complete and total truth?" T'He asked.

"But not this truth at this time. This truth will get you arrested and thrown into the prime minister's secret dungeon. Who knows when, if ever, this truth can safely be told? Have I made myself clear?" K'Too responded.

"Yes, you have, and we understand," they whispered back to her.

"Good, Sobeit," Officer K'Too stated loudly.

"Sobeit," the other students, including T'Roo, replied in unison.

"Good. That's that. Now I will leave you young ladies to get back to the rest of your scheduled classes. Do not forget what I told you before."

All too soon, the students were dismissed by Officer K'Too Ko. As soon as the last student had left, she called for F'Ree, D'Con, and both the other dorm mentors to report on what they from the students. All three claimed to report the same thing, that when they tried to find out what the students saw through the spyglass, all the students claimed to be loyal followers of Our Holy God and Blessed Father, Ablo, whose word is holy and precise beyond measure.

"It is indeed fortunate for us at Saint I'Bar College that these students do appear to comprehend that truly believing in Our Holy God and Blessed Father, Ablo, is the wise course of action; indeed, that it is the one and only path to salvation," Officer K'Too concluded before having to leave to post her report.

All too soon, suppertime rolled around. And D'Ato, D'Lir, T'Roo, T'He, and L'Rom had to decide where to eat and with whom, L'Ree, T'Alo, F'Lin, V'To, K'Amo, and D'Lo.

"Should we eat together or separately? Either way, I fear we will be watched?" T'He questioned.

"Well, we might as well eat together, because if we are going to be watched regardless, then we might as well keep it easy for them," D'Lir concluded.

"Yes, might as well. As soon as word gets out, no one will want to eat with us anyway, so we might as well stick together," T'Roo concluded.

The next day, the students walked into Professor O'Well's freshmen Science class. They saw a strangely familiar man writing something on the board.

CHAPTER 8
THE NEW NORMAL BEGINS

For T'Roo, L'Ree, V'To, and T'He, their football class began in near silence, with their classmates whispering and pointing at them. "Class, line up on this line. You should know how to do it. You have done this before. Come on, the sooner we pick sides, the sooner we can get the game started," the professor said. Four of her students lined up, but the others were reluctant to do the same. "What is the meaning of this? Line up like you did yesterday!"

The class did as they were told. After counting off by twos once again, T'Roo and V'To found themselves playing against L'Ree and T'He. Soon all those in the class were too focused on the game to think about anything else, only that the team with L'Ree and T'He won, beating the other team without the vest three to two.

"Welcome, class. I am not sure if any of you remember me from the Freshmen Dinner, but I am Professor O'Bar Skro. I will be taking over all of Professor O'Well's Science classes, including this one, since it would appear he will not be returning to teaching this year," he said. As the students begin to take their seats, he continued, "Since this class lost more class time than any of his other Science classes, we will have to work hard to make up lost time. Thus, for the next few days, you will have to endure more homework than usual, until this class is caught up to where it should be. So how much of chapter one did Professor O'Well cover?"

"What about Professor O'Well?" D'Lir asked. "None of us remember him being sick."

"Never mind about Professor O'Well. His health and well-being are now in the hands of and Our Holy God and Blessed Father, Ablo. He would no doubt want his class to continue without him," Professor O'Bar responded sternly.

A male student spoke up. "Actually, Professor O'Well did not have the chance to start any chapter before the spyglass came up. All we really had was one day of class, and then we were told we were part of an experiment to see if a destitute young person would be able to earn a scholarship here. That was all the Science class we had. Concerning the spyglass, we all looked through. Will we all be arrested or just continue to have our identifications checked and re-checked every time we come and go from our dorm buildings?"

"I would imagine that if we stopped talking about the spyglass, we would soon find ourselves all caught up. One day, when Norhem is ready to hear what you saw, you will all be writing books about it, but until that day comes, my job is to see that you all not only live to see the end of this school year but also graduate to the next level. If I have made myself clear, can we move on?" Professor questioned in a stern whisper. "So, after so many days of classes, we will basically be beginning the first lesson. Well, let us finally begin." After the now-routine security checks, before and after the evening meal, just when everyone thought we could sit back, relax, and concentrate on our studies, the wail of the tornado alarm pierced the silence of that evening.

"Attention, attention! This is only a tornado drill. I need everyone to step out of their rooms and into their hallways in an orderly manner. You will calmly walk down one of the two centrally located staircases. Either my assistant, D'Con, or an upperclassman volunteer will point you in the right direction, or I will lead you personally. No pushing, no shoving. There is plenty of room and plenty of time. This is only a drill. I need everyone to stay calm as you keep the various lines moving," F'Ree announced. Of course, the students whose parents paid for the first-floor privileges were the first to arrive, as usual.

"What steps?" The students from the first-floor dorm room asked.

"The steps that lead to the tornado shelter. Follow me," F'Ree said as she led the students down the stairs.

Soon it was T'Roo's and D'Fro's turn to walk down the well-lit stairway. As she was walking, T'Roo pondered, *This is strange. The upper stairways were all so well lit up with emergency lighting lest anyone trip and fall. But these basement stairs are lit only on this side. It looks like there is another wall on the other side, but it is so dark, one can hardly tell what is on the other side of the stairway. I wonder why—or if this is yet another case of "Why ask why?" After all, all these railings along the stairs are so plain, but those railings that lead from the stairs to the tornado shelter are so decorated. Interesting. I wonder why.*

"I most certainly hope that this tornado drill does not take too long. We all have our studies to get back to," D'Fro complained. "Well, at least there is one bright side to this drill: only those who are in the building can see me now.

Thankfully, these other women can see me in my curlers all they want, just as long as there are no tall, handsome eligible men in the group.

"But, what would happen, Ablo forbid, if a tornado struck during the day, while the groundskeepers were still working? Where would they go for shelter?" T'Roo asked.

"Someplace else, I would imagine. After all, they may not be in this shelter, but I would imagine there would be a shelter for even them," D'Fro answered. "Now, enough about them. This may be our one and only drill before the real thing strikes. Pay attention to what you need to know to save yourself lest your ignorance should cost a life, especially if that life is mine."

As the room with the four rows of benches continued to fill up with students, more and more came in to sit down.

"All right, ladies, this is where everyone in this building, or near this building, sits and waits during a tornado warning. During the tornado watch, it is your job to see that you are prepared to come down. After all, a tornado watch is not the time to decide to wash your hair, because you never know when a watch may turn into a warning, and by the time you have finished doing your hair, you just may find that was the last thing that you have done in this life," Free said. "Where was I? Oh, yes. This is where you wait for the bell to ring. That bell signals that the danger has passed and it is safe to return to your rooms." Just then, the bell rang. "Hear that? That is what you want to hear. Now, ladies, I want to see the same orderliness that brought everyone here. Take everyone back to your rooms. After all, if no one pushes or shoves, then we will all make it back to our rooms. Have I made myself clear?" F'Ree said.

"Yes, F'Ree," they all said in unison. One by one, they stood up and walked out.

T'Roo stopped at the railing and said, "I wonder what is on the other side."

D'Fro replied, "Who knows, and who has time to care? There are ladies behind us who want to get back to their dorms, even if you want to take your good old time. Long story short: now is not the time to worry about nonsense." She pushed T'Roo back as she passed by her. After everyone got back to her own dorm room, D'Fro asked, "Where do you think you are going?"

"To the music building to practice. After all, I promised that I would make our ensemble the best string ensemble here, so I have to get at least one hour of good, solid practice in," T'Roo answered.

"If you are like me, this drill kept me from finishing my homework. Did you finish yours?" D'Fro asked.

"No, but I can do my homework later, which is more than I can say about practicing," T'Roo explained.

"Just remember one thing: while you are doing your homework later, you had better not even think about disturbing my beauty rest," D'Fro warned. "Good luck with your music, and good night."

* * *

The next day, as F'Ree was driving to Prime Minister E'Li Shro's palace, she worried about how she would explain that she did not know anything about the timing of Professor O'Well's science class. Nor did she have any idea about the item they were testing or for whom the spyglass was being tested. In fact, to this very moment, she had no idea who had sent the spyglass to the professor for testing, to see if the invention could earn that someone a scholarship to attend Saint I'Bar College. She began to fear that the price she would pay for this lapse of intelligence information might be her very life, and she wondered whether they would hang her or throw her into the dungeon or worse: accuse her of being a spy and not only question her accordingly but also start a more thorough study of her activities and, worse, do a thorough search of her background.

F'Ree lifted the oversized iron ring that hung from this monstrous beast's iron fangs as she knocked on the palace door. The sound of the solid cast-iron object striking the solid wooden door could be heard far and wide, a sound that was so big and loud that anyone who dared approach would feel small in contrast, including F'Ree, especially under these circumstances. The butler opened the door to let her in as usual, but this time he informed her, "Good evening, Miss F'Ree Fo. You are most certainly expected."

The private secretary greeted her next. "Miss F'Ree Fo, you had better have the most excellent explanation for this most grievous error in judgment. After all, was it not you who said there was nothing to fear from this class? Not only that, but the prime minister is most displeased, to say the least, that you claimed you could not make it here yesterday?"

"The dorm had its first tornado drill," F'Ree explained.

"Is that the best you can do?" he questioned.

"Where else would the dorm advisor be during their first tornado drill—especially since I am the dorm advisor to the freshmen girls' dorm? Or am I to confess that I secretly work for the prime minister?" F'Ree countered.

"We will have to wait and see what the prime minister has to say about that excuse. If your punishment were up to me, I would have demanded your promptness much sooner, or at least demanded a better excuse for your tardiness. This begs the question: Why did you not know what Professor O'Well Thro's Science class was up to? And why didn't you know anything else about their activities? Should that not be considered a major security breach? How are you going to attempt to explain all of that away?"

"Can anyone here in Prime Minister E'Li Shro's palace name or even begin to count how many inventions, essays, songs—both newly composed and performed, as if a student who can play a musical instrument or sing should be worthy of a scholarship—not to forget all the other materials, that flood into Saint I'Bar College? Each and every day, more and more would be students keep trying to earn a scholarship and their parents, who volunteer to do free work, with the same goal in mind? If anyone here can, then you are correct to say that I was derelict in my duties. If you cannot, then you are as fallible as I am," F'Ree countered, summing up all her courage and composure.

Prime Minister E'Li Shro announced his presence in the room, saying, "I fear Miss F'Ree is quite correct in this case."

"If that is true, then what can be done to keep anything like this from happening again?" the private secretary, E'Lam, questioned.

"Good question, nephew. Good question. According to the law, everything that comes in is supposed to be reviewed by the minister of education, but for one reason or another, this professor decided to examine it himself before sending it off to the ministry. It is no surprise, since sadly, so many families still have a misconception that if they win over a professor or two, they will have a better chance than others to get a scholarship for their offspring. This is false, but so many families feel the need to believe it anyway. The best resolution we have come up with so far is to continue to make it perfectly clear that only the minister of education can award any scholarship to any college. After all, if potential students stop sending their entries to the colleges, then professors won't be tempted to study them before sending off them to the ministry," Prime Minister E'Li stated.

"Which still leaves one question unanswered, should Professor O'Well's students ask. Where is Professor O'Well now?" F'Ree asked.

"Should any ask, simply tell them that he fell ill from exhaustion and chose to retire in order to rest up. If they persist in asking, simply take their names and inform me as soon as possible who they are."

Prime Minister E'Li concluded the briefing. As F'Ree drove away, she remained hypervigilant to ensure she was not being followed. She had yet another stop to make before returning to her college boarding room. She parked her motor cart alongside the mountain barrier and thought, *Oh, how I hope and pray the rain holds off until after I finish what needs to be done. Then again, I always keep a spare pair of shoes in the motor cart at all times for just this type of emergency. I should be grateful these mountains stand all those thirty thousand some odd feet into the air and then some, which is why no one expects anyone would climb them, but I cannot allow that to give me a false sense of security. At any time, I may still be caught, and both sides still chop the heads of spies.* She used a blue light to identify the correct fake rock, which she lifted up and off.

There, on a mountainside covered in creeping white thyme, she revealed a hidden mailbox. She placed her note there before driving away as fast as she could.

Not long after that, a figure climbed from the fake boulder that led to a tunnel from So'hem, opened the other fake rock, and retrieved the note left in the mailbox. It read:

Do not be concerned about the Professor O'Well affair, which is strictly a Norhemian Internal Affairs matter. It has nothing to do with So'hem or the power plant that they are building.

*   *   *

At yet another Beta String Ensemble's group practice sessions, the practice went on as usual, until the music director himself walked in.

"Greetings, sir. You honor us with your presence. May I inquire about the reason for this visit? I hope we have done nothing wrong. After all, it is a rare day indeed for the music director himself to be here in person," the alto lyre player said.

"It is my honor to be here. After monitoring the practice sessions of all the string ensembles, it has come to my attention that it is you, the Beta String Ensemble, who would best represent Saint I'Bar College." The room erupted in joy, until he continued, "Sadly, I also have some less-than-good news. It has been determined that one of your Norhemian lyre players will have to be replaced with another, or else the Beta String Ensemble forfeits its privilege."

"Then we won't play," the backup alto lyre, the backup Norhemian lyre, and the bass lyre players all said in unison.

"Think about it. I will be back when you have reached a decision," the music director said as he left.

"Hold it! How dare you! This is my senior year. T'Roo is only a freshman. She will have many opportunities to play the national anthem at many other venues. This may be one of my last opportunities to cap off my many years of college on a high note. So how dare you be so willing to forfeit this opportunity for me?" the lead alto lyre player scolded. "Then again, how could the rest of you understand? Among the three of you, there are two sophomores and one junior, which means you will have many more opportunities to play at other venues. But just imagine if this was happening during your senior year. Would you be just as willing to forfeit this opportunity then?"

Silence filled the room.

The bass lyre player said somberly, "I am sorry, T'Roo, but she really does have a point—not that this is fair to you, either."

"Well, how about this? If T'Roo agrees to step aside this time, then she will have the right to play lead the next time we get called on to play the national anthem, no matter how much rewriting we have to do?" one of the lyre players suggested. Everyone nodded in agreement.

"I do not know how that will work out, but I guess I can go for that. If you must go on without me, I guess you must," T'Roo said. She began to pack up her lyre.

The music director returned as T'Roo picked up her lyre case. "So, it is agreed. I will be right back with your new, and very temporary, Norhemian lyre player."

As he walked out the door, T'Roo was right behind him. T'Roo turned around to say, "Well, for all of your sake, I do hope it goes well for all of you at the Grand Opening."

"Again, we are all very sorry that it worked out this way, but thank you, thank you for being so understanding," the alto lyre player said. "Don't forget, we will make this up to you, one way or another. This we swear on the *Sacred Book of Ablo*."

T'Roo turned around and walked out of the practice room. News that either she is replaced by the Alpha String Ensemble's Norhemian lyre player or the Alpha String Ensemble will replace them.

CHAPTER 9
THE OPEN HOUSE

As the weather continued to grow cooler, the days shorter, and the nights longer, the freshmen students were woken up one morning by the usual call-to-worship bell. Each and every student repeated the morning chant three times. This included T'Roo and D'Fro, who chanted in unison, "All good, faithful, obedient, and fruitful believers who have served well will live richly rewarded in peace and rest with the Almighty and Holy God, Our Blessed Father, Ablo. Sobeit, Ablo, Sobeit."

However, today, F'Ree added, "Today, following breakfast will be Saint I'Bar College's day for all the science classes to tour the new power plant that is about to go into operation. Be advised that mass public transportation will be provided for each science class as long as every student arrives at the designated bus stop at the proper time. Students should be prepared for a half-hour drive to the power plant, at least a one-hour tour of the plant, and finally another half-hour bus ride back to the college. Complete details will be on the assignment sheets posted in the cafeteria. The professors can only travel there with their first class and are expected to ride back along with their last class."

After breakfast, T'Roo read, made notes, and pondered, *So, my science class has been scheduled to gather at the Science building at the time I would usually be finishing Physical Education. I don't mind missing Physical Education, but this means I will also be missing History class. That means more studies I'll have to catch up on once again. I swear, keeping up with all these studies is oh so much harder than anyone ever said it would be. To be honest, this college is making it harder than it should be, but who am I to say? I am a mere freshman. All I can say is that this field trip had better be worth it.*

As the time approached for Professor O'Bar Skro's Science class, all were there as F'Ree read off the list of names. She announced to all present in the Science class that they had been one of the lucky classes selected to attend the first day of the power plant tours. She also reminded them that he would be waiting for them over there. "Why are all the Science classes required to take this trip? It feels like I have just caught up with my science lessons," one female student complained.

F'Ree quietly sighed and said, "Just get inside and don't argue about it."

As they were taking their seats, the murmurings persisted.

"I wonder, does anyone else question whether I'Mar's family is really as successful as he dresses? After all, we only wore our dress skirts to the Freshmen's dinner, and all he seems to have to wear are dress skirts. Does anyone else find that peculiar?" one student whispered.

"No. I for one have more important things to worry about than what other guys are wearing," E'Bar snapped back.

"Good question. I was wondering that exact same thing for the exact same reason myself," T'Roo, who was sitting next to her, responded. "I just hope it's at least half as educational as they say it will be, but I have my doubts, since I have no plans whatsoever in majoring in Science."

"Me neither. If you ask me, History is far more fascinating," D'Lir concluded.

"I don't understand. Is Professor O'Well still in the hospital or what? After all, the night we were testing the spyglass, he seemed so very healthy," E'Bar questioned.

"But if Professor O'Well did not suddenly take ill—quite suddenly, too suddenly, in fact. My father's a doctor. I got in touch with him, and he said that the exhaustion takes time to work up to, even for an older man. But then again, why else would they take him away?" I'Mar countered. A deafening silence overtook them, since no one, absolutely no one, was permitted to question the church authority on anything, not even the prime minister.

To break the silence, E'Bar said, "At least, thanks to Professor O'Bar, we are permitted to continue our education, as sure as we have Our Holy God and Blessed Father to thank for Archadea, Norhem, and our very lives. Thanks to the amazing grace of Our Holy God and Blessed Father, Ablo, Sobeit."

The others around E'Bar repeated, "Sobeit," which became a verbal wave that swept throughout the vehicle.

Soon the class arrived at the new upcoming power station, as they got off the bus, they were greeted by Professor O'Bar, who, with one of the engineers of the power plant, prepared for their tour to begin. "First, permit me to introduce myself. I am Doctor E'Mitt Kro. I have designed this power plant to have the capability of supplementing the other power plants with enough electricity that power outages will become a thing of the past. As we all know from experience, with the days getting shorter and shorter, more and more lights are turned on in homes and offices earlier and earlier, thus triggering even more power outages, which this power plant was designed and built to end. One day, you will tell your grandchildren that when you were young and electric lights were still such a new invention, the lights would go out at the most irritating hours and frequencies. You could almost come to expect it when you least expected it. Good news: those days are about to end. Because unlike the other power plants, which lose power as the electricity moves down the wires, this power plant will not, and when these currents merge into one, all the problems we have ever had with power outages will end."

"Yes, class, but first, let us thank Doctor E'Mitt Kro and all those responsible for the building of this power plan, especially our prime minister, who is ultimately responsible for the government funding of such a project and for giving us a preview of how it will operate even before it is in actual operation," Professor O'Bar said.

"Actually, Professor O'Bar and students, it is to our mutual benefit that we introduce you to the facility before it is in actual operation. Like the other power plants, once it is fully operational, it will also become near deafeningly loud. In addition, for some unknown reason, power plants become dustier and dirtier than mere logic can explain. One day, that problem will become your generation's job to solve.

Right now we use methane gas, which by itself very clean, to turn the turbines that generate the electricity. Also, all factories, especially power plants, become unbearably hot once they are fully operational. Yet this is also why we need another generation of engineers: the challenge of how to create an engine that does not generate heat. Who knows? Perhaps someone from any of these Science classes will be the person to solve that problem. However, most important of all, whether or not the problem is solved, one thing is almost guaranteed to happen: one day, it will be your generation's turn to maintain and operate all these power plants you are inheriting. Whether you keep them or replace them will be up to you, just as our previous generation switched over to methane gas when there were no longer forests to provide the lumber to burn to generate electricity," Dr. E'Mitt explained.

"Excuse me, but I beg to differ. After all, at our college, we have many gardens that contain trees. So how can you say that we no longer have logs to burn to generate electricity when there are so many gardens around?" a student questioned.

"Certainly by now all you students should know that Our Holy and Blessed Father, Ablo, gave us the authority over all her creation. We used the creation that was once called the Forests of Norhem to the fullest extent. In addition, she also gave us the beasts of the field. Those which we found to be useful, we have used, and we have done away with those that we found unusable to our needs or wants. In the course of time, she gave us methane gas, which can be most easily found near our old landfills, to replace the trees not only for our heating needs but also to generate electricity. Thus, we have eliminated our need for forests, which were far different from the one or two trees you now find in various gardens. Now do you understand the difference?" Dr. E'Mitt explained.

A loud hush overtook the students. No one dared to ask any more questions for now. "Since there appear to be no more questions, let us begin our tour," Dr. E'Mitt Kro stated. He opened a set of metal doors that led a room full of generators standing on concrete floors. E'Mitt Kro pointed out, "Once you start studying the old generators, then you will learn how these generators are more efficient than ones from previous generations."

"Why is that?" D'Lir asked.

"This is due to updated engineering techniques and advances in electro-physics, which, thanks to our prime minister, are included in our national budget."

"The bigger question is how can anyone stand working here with all this stink?"

"Please forgive the fishy smell. Even though the machinery is not in operation yet, they must be thoroughly lubricated so they can go straight into operation. Until someone invents an oil that can keep the machinery going as well as fish oil does, one must learn to ignore the smell. I have worked in various power plants for so long now that ignoring the smell is second nature to me. Thus far, it has been proven that keeping all types of machines lubricated is absolutely necessary to prevent them from becoming a lump of melted metal. Come to think of it, this could be another invention for your generation: invent a lubricant that works as well as fish oil but without the stink."

"With all due respect, sir, is it indeed wise to have a concrete floor over a basement? After all, over time, concrete may become too heavy for the basement walls to continue to hold up," I'Ram questioned.

"Actually there are two basements, but that is a good question. What you are really describing is not an increase in weight but the stress of persistent weight, such as the persistent dripping of water that eventually wears away a great and mighty stone. However, students, do not concern yourselves that stress will take down this building. The engineers were careful. They not only created a stronger and lighter concrete but also, when they chose the proper thickness of it, they carefully created a mixture that was strong enough to support the constant weight and vibrations of the generators yet light enough not to cause a cave-in. That is also why both basements' walls are also reinforced with even stronger concrete, especially the sub-basement," E'Mitt explained.

"Will we be going into the either or both of the basements ourselves to see the walls?" another student asked.

"I see no reason not to, even though I must warn you, once you have seen one methane gas tank, you have seen them all to one degree or another. The only variation, if you can call it that, is in size and holding capacity," Dr. E'Mitt responded.

As they approach the basements, one of the workers passed them as he walked through the basement swinging door, causing the students to gasp in amazement.

"Oh, yes, I have forgotten. All the doors you have ever seen in your young lives have always opened in one direction or the other. This one indeed opens in both directions, to accommodate both those going to and coming from the basement speedily. That is also why the door is made out of steel pipes, seven vertical and four horizontal—so that workers can clearly see if someone else is also approaching the door. This is not only a safety measure, because of all the accidents at the expense of training new workers, but it is also a cost-cutting one, since this door requires less building materials to craft out," Doctor E'Mitt explained.

"This begs the question: When two workers arrive at the door at the same time, who decides who goes first?" I'Mar asked.

"There are no real hard and fast rules per se, but everyone is expected to put their faith in action by serving the managers and the elders of the company first, especially the senior management. All praise be to Our Holy Almighty God and Blessed Father, Ablo, Sobeit and Sobeit," Doctor E'Mitt said. Everyone joined in on the second Sobeit.

"Thank you, Doctor E'Mitt for reminding us all of the blessed benefits of following Our Holy God and Blessed Father, Ablo," Professor O'Bar said. "Lead on, Dr. E'Mitt, lead on."

The students followed the doctor and their professor across the landing, which was barely lit by a solitary ceiling lamp, and down the cold hard concrete stairway surrounded by even colder and darker bricks with only metal hand railings to hold on to on their way down.

"T'Roo, is it just me, or does this stairway remind you of the stairway that leads to the tornado shelter in our dorm," T'He whispered.

"Well, I guess it does in some ways, even though there are two basements here," T'Roo whispered back.

"Welcome. Here you have it, in many ways the heart of the operation. These are the gears that move the belt, which moves the copper wires around the magnets that generate the electric current. The energy to move the gears is the methane gas that is stored in the lower basement," Doctor E'Mitt pointed out. He added, "When all eleven of these new improved and enlarged mega-generators are working in harmony, power outages will be a thing of the past. Any questions?"

Dr. E'Mitt and the professor led the students down the other flight of stairs to the sub-basement, where the methane gas was stored. There was an awkward silence, until Professor O'Bar spoke up. "Since no one has any questions for the good Doctor E'Mitt, I believe the best thing you students can do is to return to the college. I would image most of you are getting rather hungry about now."

"That does sound like a very good idea," Doctor E'Mitt said. "I believe I just might have time for a meal break myself. Good day, class. I do hope at least a few of you will consider studying this science of electricity. After all, there are still so many advances yet to be made and so many questions yet to be answered about it."

That evening, as her string ensemble held their final practice, T'Roo was told that she would be replaced since no one from her Science class had earned back that much trust. She asked why they took so long to tell her. She was told that it was convenient to keep her practicing for the event so that her whereabouts could be easier to track.

*   *   *

At one of the many churches in the college, the young man O'Kar came in, very dirty and very sweaty. As he attempted to walk past the church service and straight to the charity kitchen, he was stopped.

"Hold it right there! Who do you think you are coming to church looking like that?" O'Ron yelled out.

"I am O'Kar, son of K'Ree. I just moved into my own apartment, which I can barely afford. I lost my job for a while, but I got a temporary job clearing ditches, which was closer to this church than my apartment, so I came straight here," the young man explained.

"Well, didn't anyone, especially your mother, ever explain to you that this is a house of worship? We do not have shower facilities here. However, the men's restroom does have a sink. Go there and see what you can do to make yourself presentable, as quickly and as neatly as possible," O'Ron said.

"Yes, sir. I will or should I call you Mister O'Ron? I believe you are the one whom my mother told my all about. I understand you are the one who is really in charge of the church's charity outreach," O'Kar said before. He began walking away.

"So why did you move out if you could not afford to live on your own?" O'Ron asked.

"For a while, I could afford it, but then I got fired. I am nineteen years old. How can I move back home with my mother? We have both had a taste of freedom now, I the freedom of doing what I want and when I want, without answering to anybody, and she, no doubt, the freedom of not having to clean up after anyone but herself," O'Kar answered. "As I was about to say, I could barely afford the apartment, so I bought what food I could afford for breakfast and even less for lunch. As you have already stated, getting cleaned up should be my first priority. By the way, if I get cleaned up fast enough and well enough, can I please eat before the service so I do not faint from hunger during the service?"

"You know very well that that goes against church policy. Too few would stay for church service after they have eaten their fill. But I can see that you are indeed desperate. I will see if the kitchen will fix you a small bite to eat to at least keep you from disturbing the service," O'Ron offered.

After O'Kar ate his sandwich, church service and the charity meal went on as usual.

* * *

That night, as the prime minister and his wife were asleep in bed, a clap of thunder woke them both up.

"What was that?" he exclaimed as both were jarred awake from a sound sleep. "I do believe that was thunder. Listen to that rain on the roof. I declare, I have never heard it rain like that before. Have you?" the prime minister asked.

"No, I have not," his wife said in stunned disbelief, her eyes fixed on the ceiling as if she could look through the ceiling to the roof.

A lightning bolt, followed by another deafening ground shaking clap of thunder, confirmed the answered that question. "Dear, if it is raining this badly tonight. How can there be a Grand Opening for our new power plant?" his wife asked.

"I don't know, but I fear if it does not open on schedule, the voters will blame me. That is exactly why I cannot afford to go back to sleep. If you need me, I will be in my office. I have the sad duty to wake up the others so that the Grand Opening will be on schedule—or at least as close to it as possible," the prime minister answered.

CHAPTER 10
THE BIG DAY

T'Roo, silent and somber, was one of many students who had once again returned to her semi-usual schedule, but today breakfast was canceled to the delight and celebration of most of the student body. This was due to the radio broadcast of the Grand Opening of the New Power Plant. Prime Minister E'Li began the proceedings by introducing himself.

"Ladies and gentlemen and the good people of Norhem, permit me the honor of introducing the holy man next to Our Almighty, All-Knowing, All-Powerful True God of gods, Our Holy God and Blessed Father, Ablo's, own heart. This holy man has continually served Our Holy God and Beloved Father, Ablo, for nearly forty years now and counting, the last seven as the high cleric of Norhem. Yet he insists that he is not worthy to be called a saint. Even so, let us welcome the High Cleric O'Lam as he is about to lead us personally in the invocation."

In the dining hall Saint I'Bar College and throughout the campus thereof to every shire of the nation of Norhem, all within hearing range of a radio stood in solemn reverence as Saint I'Bar College's Beta String Ensemble played the

National Anthem. T'Roo, who stood there by herself, was particularly attentive.

Amid the applause, the master of the ceremony said, "Yes, yes, let us thank the Beta String Ensemble of Sain I'Bar College over there in West Shire for the faithful service to Our Holy God and Blessed Father, Ablo, and to our nation, whom Our Beloved God, Ablo, has most certainly blessed. Now I ask for everyone to continue to stand for the opening prayer, which the High Cleric O'Lam himself will lead. So, let us give a warm welcome our high cleric, upon whom Our Holy God and Blessed Father, Ablo, has bestowed the worldly leadership of his church."

"Thank you. Now I ask that you all remained standing with heads bowed," High Cleric O'Lam began. "Almighty Ablo, You are our one and only True Creator and Sustainer. You are our one True Light and Fortress. You are our True Wisdom and Strength, who inspires us to be strong enough to be our wiser selves. We thank you for your guiding hand that led us through the planning and building of this power plant, which only serves to light our way to you as we continue to meditate on your written word throughout our evenings, no matter how long those evenings may become throughout our year. May we approach the day-to-day operation of this power plant with wisdom, knowing that the small light that it takes to read your word is only a pale one compared to your abundant and glorious light of love. May our conduct continue to create an environment of cooperation in mutual service for the common good. Thank you, Our Holy God and Blessed Father, Ablo, without whom nothing would be possible, for helping us accomplish our work this day. We ask all these things in your all-powerful name, Most Holy,

Most Loving Blessed Father, Ablo, without whom we would not be here. Sobeit."

Each student repeated, "Sobeit." The student body and others then went back to what they were doing or about to do. T'Roo finished her breakfast and walked away from the table.

As the day continued, all too soon, T'Roo returned to the dining hall for lunch, just in time for the live radio broadcast of Prime Minister E'Li Shro's speech, she walked as he was saying, "Today, I welcome all who have joined us here on this grand occasion, be it live and in person or in spirit, by way of the radio waves. Today, I speak not as your prime minister but as a fellow citizen who has endured many a power outage while reading and studying Ablo's Holy written word."

"D'Fro, please pass the gravy?" T'Roo asked.

"All right, here it is. But we really should be listening to our prime minister!" D'Fro scolded.

"Why? If you have heard one political speech, you have heard them all. Besides, I am hungry." T'Roo poured her gravy on her food and continued, "Don't forget, we will have classes, which should be all about his speech and that grand new power plant, which means instead of advancing our studies, all we will get is even more homework—all so that we do not fall behind while we are being distracted by our prime minister's speech. Not to mention they will probably be rebroadcasting his speech for the rest of the night."

"You have a point there, but then again, this is historical. One day, we will be tested on how much we remember about this event, be it historically or scientifically. It would appear that I have already offended far too many professors and most certainly more than enough classmates. This would be a nice, easy way to win back some goodwill," D'Fro said. T'Roo waved her goodbye and left.

*   *   *

At the newly-named Prime Minister E'Li Shro Power Plant, after the prime minister under whose term it was conceived, funded, and built, one by one, each generator went online. As this began, the crowd dispersed, leaving the honored guests, invited guests, and various reporters to return to their own schedules, each person presuming all the action had already happened and it was now down to the new routine.

"Miss F'Ree, it was a splendid Grand Opening ceremony and most enlightening, was it not?" one of the deans said. "We were so blessed to be among the few honored guests to sit with both the prime minister and the high cleric himself, were we not?"

"Yes, it was. It was a splendid Grand Opening and a privilege to be among the honored guests," F'Ree said. "Is there anything else I can do for the college president or his family, or you or your family, or the other deans or any of their families?"

"Thank you but no thank you. By the way, did you happen to notice that not only did Prime Minister E'Li Shro come up to greet us, but so did High Cleric O'Lam himself? They thanked us at I'Bar College for all we do to advance Norhemian culture throughout Archadea," another dean pointed out with great pride.

"I confess that I must have missed that part since my attention was elsewhere at the time. However, I am not surprised, considering Saint I'Bar College grand reputation," F'Ree said. "Indeed, as I was saying, I would venture to say that you have completed your assignment quite well. No matter how big of a target this power plant has become, they can handle their own security from here on. Therefore, I believe we should all go back to our own lives and finish our day as each of us sees fit to do. By the way, E'Lo Dro, the minister of West Shire, has graciously invited the president of I'Bar College and myself, along with various other college deans, to his office to discuss future plans for our college's expansion—a discussion I assume you will not find interesting—so I bid you a blessed good day," the dean said. Then he rushed to join the others.

"Good day," F'Ree said as she waved good-bye to the others just before she walked over to her motor cart and drove away. She drove for a while. Then, to her surprise, her motor cart suddenly stopped. *Her first thoughts were What the — just happened here? I have had all kinds of mechanical problems with motor carts before, but none has ever just up and died like this. Oh great! Of all the places for this to have happened, why here? I hope nobody sees me here. How will I ever explain myself?* She turned the key over and over again and again, but for one reason or another, she could not get the engine to restart. As she continued to try again and again, she felt the tension in her body rising. Suddenly she noticed, *I am out in the open, but it feels like I am suffocating, and why has the air become so sterile? I should be smelling the flowers. I should not be having this much trouble simply breathing. Oh no. Why are my joints swelling up? One thing I know for sure is that I must get to the secret mailbox. I must drop off my note … I must, I must, if it is the last thing I do.*

* * *

At I'Bar College, the day continued mostly as usual. That is, until D'Fro saw a sad-looking T'Roo and a bewildered D'Lir looking for a table. D'Fro decided to join them.

"Hold it. Why are we just standing around, holding these heavy trays, just looking at tables, when we should be sitting down and eating?" D'Fro asked.

"We are looking to sit as far away from any the speakers as possible," T'Roo answered.

"Hold it, T'Roo. The national anthem is over and done with. No, you were not treated fairly, but get over it. Besides, did you or did you not say that your ensemble promised to make it up to you?" D'Fro said.

"Yes, they did promise, and yes, I trust them to keep their promise, but I put in a lot of practice. It still hurts a bit, but that is not why I want to sit as far away from the speakers as I can. It's those speeches by all those politicians, each one trying to outdo the other in praising our prime minister. It has just gotten so very dull," T'Roo said in a very soft whisper.

"Sadly, this is the farthest table we can find, since we've already heard even the prime minister's speech too many times and don't want to hear it yet again," D'Lir said.

"Yes, this is just about the best that we can do. It appears we are not the only ones sick and tired of our prime minister's speech. But D'Fro, if you want to hear it yet again, then sit as close as you like to any one of those speakers, but please do not expect me to join you," T'Roo said.

"Oh well, I might as well sit here with you two, but just in case anyone asks, remember, we are still loyal Norhemians who feel nothing but the deepest respect and admiration for our beloved prime minister and all the good he has done and continues to do," D'Fro reminded them.

"Indeed," D'Lir and T'Roo said in unison, raising their juice glasses in a mock toast.

"But seriously, I swear, if I hear one more word about who made the dress pants that the ladies were wearing and how they looked in them or who made the dress skirts that the prime minister or any other man there was wearing, regardless of their title, I am going to scream," D'Lir declared.

"I know, I know. That's why we have an agreement to refrain from any additional comments on anyone's fashion," T'Roo said. "I wonder if that is why the high cleric and the other clerics wear those clerical robes all the time—to avoid giving anyone an opening to their fashion so they don't have to worry about having a fashion sense? Then again, most of the fashion commentary is on the women's pants, not on the men's skirts."

"So, D'Fro, have you listened to our prime minister's speech often enough to be tested on it yet?" T'Roo asked teasingly. She quickly added, "I am sorry. I could not resist the temptation. I do hope that you know that I am just joking with you. Please stay anyway. I am just learning to develop a sense of humor. After all, one thing I have definitely learned with all that our Science class has been through is that a sense of humor is one way to survive college. Oh, forgive me, I do not know if you two know each other or not. D'Fro, this is D'Lir. We are in Science class together."

"Yes, I am familiar with D'Lir. After all, we are in Language together," D'Fro said.

"We are? That is Professor O'Mar's third-period Language class," D'Lir questioned to her surprise.

"Yes, we are in the same third-period Language class. You would have been aware of this fact if you did not spend so much time questioning the professor on the requirement to know all the dialects of Norhem before moving onto Norhemian literature," D'Fro said, not bothering to hide her irritation toward D'Lir.

"Well, they do say that when words get translated over and over, they tend to see their meanings change. Something gets lost or added in the translation. So I suppose there is a certain logic to it, but D'Lir does have a point. Why should we take classes just because we are told to take them?" T'Roo questioned.

"That is it. I do not want to hear another word about why we take these classes. I just want to survive this schedule so I will be free to pick at least a few classes when I become a second-year student," D'Fro said. She continued, "Out of curiosity, which dorm room are you in, D'Lir?"

"I am on the fifth floor, room seven," she answered. "Why do you ask?"

"Like I said, just out of curiosity," D'Fro reiterated. "So that means that you are in the room right above us. We are on the fourth floor, room seven," D'Fro said.

After supper, T'Roo said, "Well, D'Lir, since we live so close, how about we all walk up those steps to our dorms together?"

"Sounds like a good idea to me. That is, unless D'Fro objects," D'Lir answered.

"No, that part I don't mind. I just wish we were free to take an elevator every once in a while. Just remember to go to your own dorm room and annoy your own roommate so that I can study in peace," D'Fro said.

"Annoy what roommate? She is rarely ever there," D'Lir countered.

"Well, I don't know about you two, but the quicker I get to our room and get my lyre, the quicker I can get at least some practice in," T'Roo said.

"I don't understand. How can you take so much time practicing your lyre and then complain that you don't have time to study? If you would just go straight to your studies, you would have plenty of time to study," D'Fro said.

"But I like playing my Norhemian lyre. It relaxes me so I can go back and do my studies," T'Roo explained.

"Fine, but that also means that no one should hear you complain about your scheduling conflicts since this is your choice that you are making. You are the one choosing to make your Norhemian lyre your priority," D'Lir pointed out.

As the three of them continued from the dining hall to their dorms, T'Roo exclaimed, "What was that and that and that?" As they each grabbed hold of each other's arms to keep from falling.

"I don't know! I have never heard thunder that loud before and never, ever three in a row like that!" D'Fro exclaimed.

"You are not joking! I have never felt thunder shake the ground like that before. I never heard it twice in a row, let alone three times. Then again, I remember lightning without thunder but never ever thunder without lightning like this," D'Lir said.

"What else could it be?" T'Roo questioned in shock disbelief. "Hold on, you two! You both look like you are swelling up. Just like my hands. I have heard stories about how loud tornadoes can be. But tornados do not do this!

Not even hurricanes do this!" D'Lir exclaimed in terror and disbelief.

"Yes, I see it and feel it too. This can't be happening," T'Roo declared in a state of total shock.

"Hold it right there! It could not have been a tornado or else the alarms would be sounding by now. I have heard many things about tornados but never ever anything about causing swollen limbs," D'Fro said.

"You're right," D'Lir said. "It probably wasn't a tornado. I don't know what it was. Nor can I think of a better place to run to than the tornado shelter. Now look, I know we all felt the ground shaking right under our feet before we felt our feet and hands and other parts of our bodies begin to swell. D'Fro, do not to forget that you almost lost your balance, just like T'Roo and I did. As I recall, we all grabbed onto each other to keep from falling."

"Hold it, you two. We are almost at our dorm building. All we have to do is climb that mountain of stairs. Is it just me or does it feel like this walk is getting longer and longer? It's as if for every step forward we take, the dorm gets moved two steps away," T'Roo complained.

"That is impossible. Buildings don't move. But I do agree, this is the same walk that we have always taken from supper, but today it is totally different. I have never felt this exhausted or out of breath. I remember arriving here back when I thought climbing those steps with two suitcases was hard, but this feels like an impossible mission," D'Lir said.

"Impossible or not, I don't think we have any other choice but to keep going and get inside. Perhaps someone inside will know what is happening to us and perhaps even cure us," T'Roo said.

As they entered their dorm room building, D'Lir asked, "Where is everybody? After all, every time I walk in, security asks me to show my photo or my hand. Every once in a while, they just call me by my full name and tell me that I can pass, not that I still look like my photo."

"I guess that is not surprising. After all, there was a time when my prints were studied every time I left the building, but that seems to have stopped. Besides, now I fear they will not be able to take my prints anymore," T'Roo said.

"I don't know what you two could have done to warrant that reaction, but it looks like I have kept my family's reputation clean, since I am always told to pass," D'Fro said boastfully.

"Well, either way, does anyone else feel like forgetting the rules and sneaking into the elevator for a ride up? After all, the way I have swollen up, I don't think I'll be able to make the walk. I, for one, would like to rest my legs and feet for a change and see if that stops this swelling," T'Roo suggested.

"Sounds good to me. I am tired of walking too. After all, there doesn't appear to be anyone here to enforce that rule. Not only that, but if we do get arrested for breaking the rules, at least then they will have to take us to get medical attention," D'Fro said.

"Make that me three." D'Lir said, half-jokingly. "If D'Fro is now willing to risk her family's good name for this ride, who am I to say no?"

"See? You two really can agree on some things," T'Roo teased them. She pushed the elevator buttons, but nothing happened.

"Now this is getting a scary kind of strange. I remember being told that we were not allowed to ride the elevator, that it was only here for medical emergencies, students arriving or leaving," D'Fro said. She added, "As bad as we feel, we have no choice but to walk up the stairs."

"Those were no tornados. I am feeling even worse than before. I don't know about you two, but I am going down to the tornado shelter," D'Lir said.

"Yes, I am beginning to think that you are right. Count me in too," T'Roo stated.

"So we have to walk instead of taking the elevator. That still does not prove a thing. Like I said before, if this were a real tornado emergency, we would be led to the tornado shelter just like we were during the drill. All I know is when there is an unsolvable mystery, the only place to turn to is Our Holy God and Blessed Father, Ablo. I'll be praying for all of us, it seems," D'Fro said. "After Ablo saves us from this, you two can tell me how much trouble you got into going on this crazy excursion."

As they entered the stairway, they saw no one, but they heard footsteps from above them. D'Fro said, "Just listen, hear that? That is the sound of everyone going back to their rooms without their imaginations carrying them away into unnecessary fear."

T'Roo and D'Lir just turned and looked at each other, nodded in agreement, and started walking down the steps anyway. As they walked, D'Lir said, "T'Roo, do you feel it too? I can feel the swelling in my hands and feet easing up. Look at my hands; they are almost back to normal."

"Yes, this must prove that we are doing the right thing," T'Roo said. The thought suddenly struck her: *Maybe, just maybe, not playing at that silly Grand Opening was the best blessing I have ever received before in my life.*

CHAPTER 11
AND SO IT BEGINS

T'Roo and D'Lir stepped into the tornado shelter. To their amazement, they were not the only ones there. A few were already there, such as L'Ree, T'Alo, D'Ato, F'Lin, L'Rom, V'To, K'Amo, and T'He, and more were walking in behind them.

"It looks like that sound didn't scare just us. Nor did we alone experience the terrifyingly strange effect of these painfully swollen limbs," T'Roo said. She breathed a sigh of relief that her hands and feet were continually going back to normal.

"No, many others got scared too, except they decided to turn to prayer instead," D'Ato responded. "What the – is happening to us?"

"Yes, this is scary and terrifying. I do not know. I am afraid that nobody knows. Nor do they know what to do about this. I remember when the glass in our window blew out. I ran as fast as I could. Why? I have no idea. I just felt like it was the right thing to do at that time. Then, all of a sudden, everything was happening in slow motion. Instead of running out with me, my roommate just dropped to her knees and started praying," T'He said.

"I have never felt a building shake like that before, and I hope I never do again," L'Ree said. The others nodded in agreement.

"It looks as if we all have experienced that same most painful swelling that coming down here has strangely cured. Which begs the question: Does anyone know what caused it all to happen and why would coming down here cured it, or should we just be happy that we were cured and not bother asking why?" D'Lir said.

"I have seen glass blow out like it did today, during a tornado, but there was no tornado, so I have no idea what caused it this time," K'Amo said.

"So we really don't know the answer to any of those questions. That raises additional questions: Are we really cured, or is it just a temporary fix?" T'Roo said. "Now that at least a few of us are here, does anyone know what we are supposed to do? Close the door or wait for the others to come—that is if anyone else arrives?" T'Alo asked as she looked around to see if anyone knew.

"No, I don't like the idea of closing the door. Who knows? Maybe at least one person might change her mind and realize that prayer is not the solution to each and every situation. Maybe it is just taking others that much longer to decide to do something else, without somebody around instructing them what to think, how to feel, and most importantly what to do," T'He said.

"But then again, if we leave the door open, we may be inviting those mysterious swellings to come back?" T'Alo countered.

"But then, if we close the door, how will F'Ree or D'Con or anyone else know that anyone is here? Holy God and Blessed Father, Ablo, forbid we are left to die here. For all we know, they may be on their way as we speak to tell us what to do," T'He replied.

Meanwhile, D'Con was looking at various screens looking for F'Ree. She pondered, *I don't understand. I have been down here all day. I have yet to go through what those people are going through. It is almost as if Our Holy God and Blessed Father, Ablo, is protecting me and only me for one reason or another. I should be thankful, but all that does is raise questions. Why me? What have I done to be found worthy of this honor? Since I have yet to find F'Ree, does this mean that she was found to be unworthy, that I merely have yet to find her, or what?*

As she viewed the screen from their very own rooftop, she saw the workers, whose entire bodies had swollen up but whose job it was to maintain the roof, react as if they were suffocating to death. At the sight of that, she determined that under these unconventional circumstances, she must forego doing the unconventional thing. As a result, she marched out of the room and up the stairs to the open door.

"Oh, D'Con, are we ever so glad to see you! What do we do? What do we do? Do we close the door or what?" T'He exclaimed as all those with her looked equally petrified.

"First, ladies, you are all going to calm down and stop panicking. I must confess that I do not have any idea what is happening here either. This has never ever happened before. This is like nothing I have ever trained for, so I must confess that this terrifies me too, but one thing I do know is that no problem ever got solved, or ever will get solved, while people are in a state of panic. Second, all but one must come with me. I may not be able to figure out what is happening up there, but if we all put our heads together, we just might be able to figure things out together. Third, about that person, I need her to be a volunteer to stay behind to direct other students, if there are any other students, into the sub-basement security room. We do not know what may happen to the person left behind here. I don't even know if anyone else will come or not, which is why I need a volunteer who can point the way through this gate and down those steps. Hopefully, F'Ree will come soon and tell us all what we should be doing, but I have no idea where she went or how long she'll be or if anything happened to her or anything. All I know is that she left earlier today, saying that she was so very glad and in such a good mood to get the assignment to watch the Grand Opening ceremony. She promised me that she would tell me all about it. She even joked that she would be there pretending to work on who was worried that Security Officer K'Too Ko was there watching them, but I haven't heard a word from her, and the ceremony ended hours ago. So now, you know just about as much as I do." D'Con explained that even though the mere thought of telling them about the worker on the roof terrified her far too much for her to even think about telling them. If she told them, she would have to speak the words out loud.

"You said that you needed a volunteer. I guess I can wait here in this doorway as well as anyone. I'll do it," L'Rom said. "But first, please explain, since I don't understand. This is the most serious situation that any of us has ever faced in our lives. But the chief of security is nowhere to be found instead of being here and taking charge."

"Actually, F'Ree outranks K'Too in some ways, since it is her job not to be seen as a threat and to gain the confidence of all the students. As far as where she is now, as I said, I have no idea. The last that I remember about her was that she accompanied some of the deans and other leaders of this college to be honored guests whose work built the power plant," D'Con explained.

"You mean the one that all our Science classes got a tour of?" V'To asked.

"Yes, that one. It is the only new power plant that has opened up lately," D'Con said, showing signs of disliking the question.

"Then all those stories are true about security officers dressed as civilians," T'Roo concluded.

"Now that we understand each other, I need everyone to come with me. Especially you, L'Rom, since you will need to know how to tell anyone else, that if there is anyone else other the F'Ree who comes down here how to work this gate. Yes, this railing is a secret gate that hides a secret room that students like yourselves were never supposed to find out about. See this latch hidden in the back? The design is symmetrical, with two animals appearing to face each other, but in between is where the gate swings open, like this," D'Con explained as she led the students down to the hidden sub-basement. L'Rom simply turned around walked over to a comfortable spot to sit and wait. She waited as close to tornado shelter's doorway as possible.

As D'Con and the students entered the sub-basement, they were amazed at what they saw and what they didn't. "What are those things?" D'Lir was the first to ask in wide-eyed wonder as she pointed at the screens. Then it dawned on her. "Hold it. Where are the food and water supplies, in case we have to stay here for days or weeks—or, worse, even longer than that?"

"Well, I might as well answer the hard question first. In case you haven't noticed, the tornado shelter is just an empty room full of benches, almost like this room, except we have a table and chairs instead. Both of these shelters were built to house everyone only temporarily. This security one, with the thought of shift changes and the tornado, with the thought, that since all the buildings were built out of stone and brick, once the tornado passed, everyone would or could return to their rooms. That is why we need F'Ree to come back and tell us what to do. Being here is only a temporary solution to an unknown problem. If this is only temporary, then we have nothing to worry about. If the situation worsens, we will need to be rescued," D'Con explained. She took a deep breath before she added, "As far as the easy question, what are these for? Security. Very few people know about this, but we have these cameras that can seemingly operate themselves and record moving images of what happens as it is happening and transmit it onto the screen. We have various hidden cameras throughout the campus. These screens show what the cameras film around this building. That is why there are only seven screens: two from the main entrance, one from both of the side entrances, and three from the rooftop."

"So how do those cameras and screens work, since they seem to be our only contact with the outside world?" D'Lir asked.

"Good question. I have no idea. I did not invent them; nor am I trained to repair them. I was only trained in how to use them," D'Con answered as she began to demonstrate what she knew about working them. She explained as she pointed to the screen, "The camera that films the east side entrance is on this screen. What we appear to see is an older woman who appears very swollen, exasperated, and barely able to move. I can barely make out her features, so I have no idea who she could be."

"Hold it. I think I know her. I can barely recognize her. After all, her face is so swollen up. I can barely see the yellow and orange of her eyes. Yet I am almost positive that that is the gardener, K'Ree. The way she is moving oh so slowly, she looks like she is in even more pain than we were in before we came down here. By Our Holy God and Blessed Father, Ablo, it looks like she's dying. We have got to get a message to her to come inside and down here, somehow, some way," T'Roo begged.

"Yes, we can, and I suppose we should. After all, it sounds like she is your friend. All I have to do is flip this switch to on. Miss K'Ree, can you hear me? Your friend, T'Roo, is going out there to get you and help you inside. We know it won't be easy, but we need you to hold yourself together until T'Roo can reach you. Just stay there. I can see that you are at the east door. If you can open the door and let yourself in, then your rescue will be that must faster, we hope," D'Con said. "T'Roo, ah be careful and be quick." D'Con reminded K'Ree, "I'm leaving you so you can focus your energy on getting inside. We will be waiting down here for the both of you."

T'Roo couldn't help but remember what and how she had felt before she had reached the tornado shelter, so she worked even harder on focusing her mind on not only getting up the first flight of steps to L'Rom as speedily as she could but more importantly making it all the way to K'Ree, no matter what might happen to her body. She met up with L'Rom, whom she told, "We have a rescue. Got to keep going." Then she struggled to keep her mind focused.

Don't stop to wait for a reply. Can't slow down. Got to keep going as fast as possible. The slowing down will happen soon enough. Must keep going as fast as possible.

As she climbed up to the first floor, she could feel her body start to swell up again. Even worse, she felt that same old ache of the swelling return to her joints, especially when she needed her hands to grab hold of the door handle and pull the door open. As she attempted to race down the eastern hallway, she felt the swelling in her body, especially in her knees and ankles. Each and every one of her toes felt the hardness of the stone tiles, ever increasing as her air continued to get thinner. Even though she was working harder to run faster, she felt as if she were running in slow motion, and getting slower. Finally she reached K'Ree, who had barely made it into the hallway. "Come on. The hallway will be the hardest part, but we can do it," T'Roo said.

"If the hallway is the hardest part, then why don't we take these stairs?" K'Ree asked, pointing to the brick wall to her right.

"But that is a brick wall—a solid brick wall," T'Roo said.

"Not, if you press that brick. No, the one to the left of that one. Press that one in, all the way in, no matter how hard or painful it may be, or else the door will not open. The one directly above that one, push it in as well. Yes, that one. Now we stand back for the brick door to open," K'Ree explained.

"So all we have to do is squeeze through this doorway, and we should begin to recover, we hope and pray," T'Roo said. They very carefully descended the spiral staircase, and that old familiar feeling of recovery swept over once again her. "So, K'Ree, how are you feeling now?" she asked.

"Better, much better. Thank you for remembering me and not leaving me behind," K'Ree said. She took off her work scarf, revealing her short graying green curly hair. "Well, it is also thanks to you that you knew of this hidden staircase. I must confess, I knew nothing about it. Nor did I even suspect anything like this," T'Roo said as she was looking around.

"Well, I am not surprised that you knew nothing about it. I must confess, I am not supposed to know about it either. A friend of mine accidentally found it and told me about it. Ever since then, I swore that I would keep a secret of how I knew of it or that I even knew of it. Rumor has it this is how security gets around without being seen and why that big rug needs to be replaced at least three times a week, each and every week of the year, whether the college is in session or not," K'Ree explained.

"Amazing! I didn't know you knew so much about the workings of this college. After all, I don't think that I have ever seen you any other place than outside in one of the gardens or around one of the gardens," T'Roo explained.

Soon, L'Rom heard a footstep, so she ran to the one and only staircase that she could see to look for them. She could not find them, which left her to question, *Was I really hearing what I thought that I was hearing?* Soon she saw the light coming out of a dark wall, as yet another secret door opened, revealing T'Roo and an older lady who was just beginning to catch her breath. "This must be K'Ree; the others told me about her. Is there anyone else with you two?" L'Rom questioned.

"I spoke with a D'Con. I know that there are others. Where are they?" K'Ree asked.

"This is the tornado shelter, but most of us are in the security room. Believe it or not, this is not just a railing. It is yet another secret passageway. Which begs the question: Are there any more?" She opened the gate for K'Ree.

"Yes, there should be at least one more secret passageway on the western entrance that should be a mirror image of the eastern one," K'Ree said. She added, "This is absolutely amazing. Those trees, those animals, look so real. They remind me of the stories my grandparents used to tell about how many forests each shire used to have. Now trees can only be found in various gardens, but once upon a time, there were forests of them, or so I have been told, where wild animals lived, before they got moved into zoos, until the zoos were closed down because there was no space for them," K'Ree stated.

"Wow! I wondered why they picked that image to hide a gate. I wonder if that is why they picked that image," T'Roo said in amazement.

"Saint I'Bar College is a very ancient institution. Some say that it goes back hundreds of years, some say even longer than that. I wonder if at the time that gate was forged that was simply a common scene, so common that no one knew that it needed to be saved," K'Ree said. "Either way, the secret security room is just down those steps. Yes, one more stairway, and then we are there. That is where we have begun to hide out while we attempt to figure out what is happening to us—or until somebody can put a stop to this. Whatever this is," T'Roo said.

*   *   *

"Greetings, Mr. O'Ron. I am back because I lost my job and the job that I almost had, clearing the ditches after last night's rainstorm dried up. My landlord signed this note of my intention to work for him, but for some unknown reason, the ditches dried up much faster than they had ever dried up before, which was something my landlord had never seen before in all his years in real estate. Not even when he was a child at his father's knee did he hear of ditches drying up this fast," O'Kar explained. "By the way, have you seen my mother, K'Ree? There is much that I would like to talk to her about. After all, for a day of light work, I feel like I have been working at least eleven days straight without rest. My joints look and feel like it, but I know that I did not, and this I cannot explain. I am hoping that, being old and wiser, she will know. If not, someone else here might know."

"What does any of that have to do with the church? After all, I am not even sure if you are entitled to eat here, since I can barely read this note that you just handed to me. It does not look like any grown man's handwriting," O'Ron complained.

"Well, that is the note that my landlord wrote. He had pains and swelling all over his hands and fingers, so he was barely able to write or do anything else with his hands," O'Kar explained.

"Be that as it may, we are only here to feed the hungry, who cannot work the many hours it would take to feed themselves and their families," O'Ron countered. "Don't forget that worship comes first, and then the meal. Maybe then you might find someone who can explain all our joint pain. That is, if we still suffer from the joint pain after worship, since I would not be surprised if there was a mass healing by Our Holy God and Blessed Father, Ablo, this evening, seeing that now is our time of need."

"Which reminds me, I know my landlord was quite angry at those who cleaned up the puddles on the roof for not coming to see him. I don't know their names, but I believe I would be able to recognize their faces if I saw them again. Would I get into any kind of trouble if I warned them to go back to the apartments and make amends with the landlord before he calls the authorities on them and finds a way not to pay them the money he owes them?" O'Kar asked.

"As long as you wait until after the worship service, you can talk to anyone about anything, as long as neither of you causes any trouble," O'Ron stated.

"The cleric said that all must come right away. Fasting and prayer are what we need most in order for Our Holy God and Heavenly Father, Ablo, to deliver us from whatever it is that has befallen us," the messenger responded. "I can't believe it. I have never seen the cleric in so much pain before."

"Attention, attention! One and all, our cleric has called us all into the sanctuary for prayer. Stop whatever you are doing and find a place at one of the kneeling pews in the sanctuary now—as in *right now*," O'Ron said. His attention then focused on O'Kar, he said, "Well, you heard, our cleric has ordered us all into the sanctuary—that includes us both. It would appear that you will have to deal with your situation later, much later."

"I don't believe this. I worked two weeks long weeks sweeping streets, after getting laid off at the other job, only to have this happen," O'Kar said.

"You can either wallow in self-pity or you can look at your situation from a heavenly perspective. Perhaps your situation is the indirect result of your parents' sin. After all, they were not married when your mother gave birth to you, thus causing her to name you after herself. You more than anyone else would therefore know where to begin in your prayers," O'Ron explained.

O'Kar and O'Ron joined the others as they walked into the sanctuary. There, each person quietly knew their place in the commoners' pew and that it was each person's job to assist in lowering the kneeling benches. Even though they were now feeling the effects of swelling and painful joints, these were members of the working class, the class of servants, who did the physical labor of Norhem.

"As I look into the congregation, I can see that Jeho's curse has indeed spread to here. I confess that there is nothing that mortal man can do about this. Even though I am in the same pain from the same curse that has afflicted us all, I am still able to stand on the promise that Our Holy God and Blessed Father, Ablo, is still ready and willing and able to save us all from any curse the Jeho would place upon us. Therefore, let us pray as we have never prayed before. Sobeit, Sobeit," the cleric stated. "I will lead the general confession. Afterward, there will be time for personal confessions, which shall be between the individual and the Lord God Ablo only. Once the healing has started, I will again lead the prayer, but this time it will be prayers of praise, full of thankfulness and gratitude. At this time, those who have not eaten can eat their fill in peace. After all, even though this is usually the time we feed the body, we all know that that is done so the body will bring the soul to Our Holy God and Blessed Father, Ablo."

"Sobeit, Sobeit!" all shouted in unison. Others murmured quietly, "Quickly, very quickly, I came so I could eat before I fainted from hunger, not to pray."

"Let us pray to Our Holy God and Blessed Father, Ablo," the cleric commanded. "O, Holy God and Blessed Father, Ablo, we call to you like the perpetual one, the omnipresent one, who is boundless in love. Yet there are times, O, Holy God and Blessed Father Ablo, when we do not recognize you in our lives. All too often, infamy clenches tightly around our hearts, and we try to conceal our true feelings even though fear makes us small. We forsake the chance to speak from our strength, such as is happening now, when doubt and fear invade our minds and our bodies. O, Holy God and Blessed Father, Ablo, we need you from sunrise to sunset. I beg that you will forgive all of our sins and deliver us from the clutches of the evil one. O, Holy God and Blessed Father, Ablo, remind us again that your holy presence is forever hovering near us and in us. Free us from scandal and self-hatred. Help us to see you in our lives, to act courageously, and to speak from our wisdom. But most of all, I beg that you will forgive all of our sins and deliver us from the clutches of the evil one …"

The cleric continued praying until he succumbed to his own suffocation. He passed out at his pulpit, and the congregation took this as their time for silent confession of their sins, until each and every one of them also succumbed to suffocation.

CHAPTER 12

THE PALACE DUNGEON'S MOMENT OF TRUTH

Prime Minister E'Li Shro stumbled down the dungeon steps, barely able to breathe and just barely holding onto the railing. His hands, feet, and entire body were swollen, making his joints not only painful but nearly useless. There in the dungeon depth, he finally caught his breath and began to feel relief from the swelling.

"Attention! Attention!" one of the guards shouted. He and the other guards snapped to attention as he continued to stare at the prime minister's swollen appearance. He feared that if he dared say a word about it, instead of guarding the prisoners, he'd become one of them.

"At ease, at ease! Better yet, just have a seat," Prime Minister E'Li said. After fully regaining his breath, he added, "I don't know what is happening on the surface of our world, but all you guards are far better off here than there."

"Yes, sir. If you say so, sir. What can I do for you, sir?" asked the very same guard.

"I am here to speak with Professor O'Well. Where is he?" the prime minister asked.

"Just go four hallways down. He's in the seventh cell on the right," the guard explained. "Why would you, sir, want to talk to that heretic? That is, if I may ask, sir?"

"I need to talk with him. I am hoping that perhaps he can explain to me why so many people of Norhem are not only experiencing swelling of the body, starting with the hands and feet, but even worse dropping dead of suffocation, beginning with those who were the highest up in their buildings. Down here, there is a relief. How or why I do not understand. After all, this cannot be Our Holy God and Blessed Father, Ablo's, judgment, since only the innocent are being punished by this plague." The prime minister added, "That is why I strongly advise everyone down here to stay down here until we find out what is happening up there." He walked away.

"Hello, Professor O'Well Thro!" he called out.

"I am here. Who wants to know?" a shattered and drained professor answered him, showing all the wear and tear on his body caused by sitting in the cold, dark, damp dungeon in cast-iron shackles all this time.

"It is I, Prime Minister E'Li Shro. Something is happening. People are dying, and no one knows why." He described once again the plight of the people and added, "My son-in-law/personal assistant was attempting to make his way to talk to our church leaders to see what they could do about this, but I fear that under these circumstances, he didn't make it. So I came here to ask you."

"Ask me what about what? Why I am in this dungeon instead of teaching or what?" Professor O'Well asked.

"I only wish and pray to Our Holy God and Blessed Father, Ablo, that I knew what I was asking. All I know is that today was the Grand Opening of our new power plant, the mega-plant that was supposed to solve all our power-outage problems. I was at the Grand Opening. Everything went well. Each new generator went online, and everything was going well. The ceremony ended on a very happy note with nothing but optimism for the future. The next things I heard were explosions and reports of that same thing happening to each and every power plant. Some guess it had something to do with the methane gas that powers all the power plants, but no one knows for sure, because not long after that, people started dying from suffocation. Some were seemingly even burnt by the air," the prime minister explained.

"I wish I could explain everything that is happening. I remember there was one scientist who theorized that electricity flowed in what he called two currents, but sadly, before he could test his theory, he was arrested for blasphemy. Then again, I remember another scientist. If memory serves me correctly, he was the very same person who invented the very first electric generator by utilizing the power of magnets. He theorized that gravity, electricity, and magnetism were connected to each other, but before he could test his theory, he too was arrested for blasphemy, even though without him, there would be no electric generators. Now I sit here in the dungeon because my class and I had the nerve to point the spyglass that we were testing into space and open our eyes to the fact that Archadea is not the center of the universe. Nor are we probably the only planet that has, or should I say that had, life on it," the professor stated.

"I don't know what to say. Every other time when something would happen, the *Holy Book of Ablo* would have all the answers, which were quick and easy. Not even the *Holy Book of Ablo* says what is happening or what we can do about it other than beg and plead for Our Holy God and Blessed Father to swoop in and save us from ourselves.

"Between the explosions I heard and the ones you told me about, we have plenty to be saved from. Our power plants are still powered by the all-too-flammable gas methane. That science was acceptable because we chopped down all our forests, leaving only a few trees in various gardens. Am I correct or not?" the professor said.

"Yes, it is the job of science to support both the church and the state," the prime minister said.

"By doing that, you hired a group of scientists who designed and built a power plant to the state's standards that fit the church's needs, regardless of the laws of science. After all, by all rights, those methane tanks should have burst into flames, but did they?" the professor questioned.

"No, they did not," the prime minister responded, "Why would that matter?"

"Because something prevented the flames; even though there were explosions, there was not a not a single fire. We all know what it takes to start a fire: it takes a heat source, which you had, a burnable substance, which you had all kinds of, and air, which apparently you did not have, or else there would have been many fires burning. The question becomes where did the air go? More importantly, why did it go? At least you generated enough power to do something," the professor pointed out.

"But that still does not explain why people's bodies are swelling up," the prime minister said.

"Who would have been free to study it?" the professor said.

"So it looks like our final lessons are, first, do not hinder the advancement of science. Second, more power does not always solve the problem of power outages."

The prime minister stepped away from the cell and sat in a far corner of the room.

* * *

A messenger from one of the chiefdoms came running to the king's castle, crying out, "Your, Highness, Your Highness! I beg to report some bad news you need to hear. There was a massive explosion at one of our power plants."

"Which one?" the horrified King A'Mar XX Shra questioned.

"The NMP Power Station of North Shire, Your Royal Highness," he answered. "After the explosion, which seemed to be somewhat minor at the time, people started to experience all kinds of bodily swellings. Not long after that, they began to suffocate. Sadly, before the plant could be evacuated, they all died, and no one has any idea why or how."

As the king listened in horror, his mind wondered, *That is the very same power plant that I authorized could steal power from Norhem's new power station. Did they find out? Is this their revenge? If so, how do we fight back, and what do I tell the people, since I have no idea how to save them. Do I confess my weakness and my guilt?*

"Your Highness, Your Highness, what shall the people do? What shall the people do? After all, what has happened inside the power plant is beginning to spread to the outside world. People are beginning to leave the area, but we have no idea how far it will spread, so we have no idea about how many people need to be evacuated," he pleaded.

"Sounds like there is nothing that I can do about it. What does the High Priestess Z'Raa have to say about what we all should do?" the king responded.

"The high priestess is calling for fasting and prayer," he answered.

"Then that is what we all should be doing. Send the word far and wide: today has become a day of fasting and of prayer, and it shall be such every day thereafter until we are delivered from this evil that has fallen upon us," King A'Mar XX declared.

Yes, my people, you shall do that while I wait to hear from my spies. I hope that they can report on a solution that we can call Jeho's salvation.

CHAPTER 13
THE DAY THAT ARCHADEA DIED

As K'Ree was lead down the stairs, she marveled, *That was a gate. If I hadn't walked through it myself, I would have sworn it was just a railing. I've known about the other secret entrances for a long time now. There were many rumors about where they led to but no real answers until now. Absolutely amazing, and these stairs—how many generations of freshmen walked right into the tornado shelter never even suspecting that there was another level underneath it?*

"Well, here we are, home sweet home, or until we find out what is going on and when we can leave, that is, if we can leave. Permit me to introduce myself. I am D'Lir Wo," she said.

"Greetings, D'Lir. Nice to meet you, even under these circumstances," K'Ree said. She added in wide-eyed amazement, "But first what are those light screens?"

"First off, how did you know about either of the secret staircases? Only security officers know about them. I was going to tell T'Roo about it, but then I figured by the time

I explained all the details about using it, that she would be taking a short-cut to a corpse," D'Con explained.

"With all the secrets being exposed, it does look like we had all better start praying for amnesty," D'Lir said.

"This just feels so right, to finally be truly open and truly honest about what I do here. I am not scared of the state nor of the college. Not even the church scares me anymore," D'Con explained. "Which reminds me, as I was about to explain about these screens. These are the hidden cameras that have been filming all around this dorm building. Over the decades, if not centuries, security has been using a device called hidden cameras to film as much as possible about all that happens around this building, displaying it on these screens. I only work this dorm building, but I would imagine that every building that has a tornado shelter has a security room underneath it. Realistically, I would be amazed if this was the only building on campus surrounded by hidden cameras or with secret passageways for use by security officers only."

"I wonder if this is what really happened to Professor O'Well?" T'Roo questioned.

"By Ablo, does this means that there is a chance that Professor O'Well never actually left the campus. D'Con, what is the truth about Professor O'Well?" D'Lir asked.

"All the information I have comes from F'Ree. She and the other security officers took care of him according to the rules, which means that they took him far away from here, which is all I can say for sure, since there are supposed to be many dungeons throughout Norhem," D'Con explained.

"Then it sounds like F'Ree is the real person in charge of security. That also begs the question: Where is she? And why isn't she here?" K'Ree asked.

"Good question. I have no idea. The last thing that I remember her telling me was how lucky and blessed she felt early this morning when she found out that her assignment was to accompany the college president and various deans to the Grand Opening of the power plant. She promised to tell me all about it when she came back, but she has yet to come back, and I fear she may never do so," D'Con answered.

"In that case, I assume that I can also ask where the other hidden cameras are located. After all, I am the gardener. I remember them attaching something to the doorways that they refused to talk about. The only thing they told me was that when I tended the flowers near them, I should imagine those objects were not there," K'Ree explained.

"Well, in that case, you know where more than half the cameras are. The other cameras are on the roof, which is why T'Roo over there begged for us to let you in," D'Con explained. She reversed the film on one of the cameras and added, "After I witnessed this tragic death of this worker, I invited these students into the security room with me. One thing that I have noticed, but can't explain, is that down here, we do not suffer the same fate as out there or up there. I don't understand how or why, but somehow it is safer down here than out there, but I am still hopeful that someone will come and explain what is happening and why. If you haven't guessed by now, that has yet to happen. Where was I? Oh yes, when they saw that you were about to suffer the same fate as the man on the roof, how could we not invite you in?"

Everyone's attention once again focused on the rooftop screens. One suddenly faded to black, but the others showed the scene from two different angles. They noticed he had been bleeding out of his mouth, nose, eyes, and ears. They watched in terror, afraid to keep watching yet even more afraid to turn away. The body suddenly exploded into small pieces and was sucked into the air that screen also faded to black.

"Oh, no! Does that mean that we are all going to die? After all, hiding down here will save us only for so long," T'Roo concluded.

*   *   *

In the meantime, as F'Ree felt the swelling of her entire body increasing, she slowed her walking with each step. Each footstep became not only more demanding but more and more painful as she worked harder and harder to keep walking. Yet she was more determined than ever to complete her final assignment, until forced to yield to the full effect of her suffocation. Her last thought was *Oh, great and mighty Jeho, save me from this, as you saved me from the orphanage after my parents died, thus giving my life purpose and meaning in service to So'hem.* There she passed out and died only feet away from the secret mailbox that she worked so hard to get to.

Not long afterward, a So'hemian man emerged from the tunnel. As he walked over to her motionless body, he too began to feel his body beginning to swell up. He decided that the worst thing that could happen to a So'hemian spy was to be caught; that was a fate worse than even death. So, despite the swelling and pain, he worked hard to pick up and carry

F'Ree back to the tunnel, but before he could pick her up, his body began to swell up, and he felt the pain of it in each and every joint in his body. This slowed him down even more, to the point where he too felt the full effects of the thinning air. He finally picked her up and managed to carry her to the hatchway. He tried in vain to lift up the secret handle since his hand could no longer work the handle to open it. As he struggled to ignore the pain of squeezing his hand under the handle to lift it in order to get back to where he came from, he too succumbed to suffocation and died right next to where he had dropped her.

* * *

"D'Con is right indeed. Now is the time to end all the secrets. After all, it looks like we are about to die together instead of with our own families. What no one here knows about me is that I was once a student here myself from a very well respected family," K'Ree confessed.

"Then how did you end up becoming a mere gardener?" D'Con asked.

"They say it was my own fault. I met a very handsome classmate my freshman year. The following year we were dating, and the year after that I was pregnant with his child. Apparently, right after I told him about our child, the college administration found out. As a result, I was immediately expelled, and my family disowned me. I did not know what to do, and since I was already expelled, there was no reason even to consider having an abortion, which I probably would not live to tell about anyway. After all, this is Norhem; not only are there laws against such surgeries, but there are false clinics where they arrest women for even thinking about doing such a thing. Therefore, all too many doctors became afraid of being arrested by a woman's boyfriend's family who found out about her abortion. After all, the best thing that could happen to these doctors would be for the woman to die before she could name them to anyone, be it her family, the church, or the law," K'Ree explained.

"Then what did you do, and was that how you became the gardener?" T'Roo asked.

"Basically, yes, that is how I became the gardener, but I am getting ahead of myself since I did not know what to do in that situation. I did the only thing that I could think of doing in that situation, and that was to return to Professor O'Well's classroom and confide in him. He agreed that abortion would be useless since my reputation was already destroyed. He pointed out that adoption was another option to raising the child, but with oh so many children and other babies up for adoption, there was no guarantee that my child would not grow up in one of those orphanages, where rumors abound of child abuse and neglect, due to the fact that far more children come in that they can hire workers to care for," K'Ree confessed, wiping away her tears as she continued, "After that, he used his connections to find me a room on campus and the job of a gardener, where my son and I still live today. That is, if my son is still alive."

"I hear that. After all, does anyone here really know with any degree of certainty that their family is still alive and well? I know I have my doubts and fears that my family is probably dead by now, and oh how I pray to Ablo that I am wrong," T'He said. The others nodded their heads in tearful agreement.

"I might as well go first. Funny, isn't it? Now, when everything is about to be lost, the truth is no longer something to be feared. I remember walking to the dorm the first day, petrified that someone might guess I was here on a scholarship and not because my family could afford to send me," F'Lin confessed.

"Family, family privileges, family obligations. According to the teachings of Ablo, the family is everything. A family is rewarded and punished together. I know because I have my own family concerns," D'Ato admitted. "What I didn't tell anyone on moving in day, and what I hoped and prayed that no one would find out, was that I took public transportation to get as close to the college as I dared to get."

"Why? After all, not all families can afford servants, but all families can afford at least one motor cart?" D'Con said.

"Not really. My parents gave up on the dream of owning a motor cart in order to save up and send all of us kids to college, starting with me. I am the oldest and the first one in my family to go to college. That was why everything that I brought here was brand new," D'Ato said. "That is also why I take Physical Education class and the other classes so seriously. The best way to help my siblings get to go to college too is if I can switch over to an athletic or academic scholarship. That is, if any them are still alive and if any of us survive whatever is happening."

"In that case, I am sorry to tell you, but since we are both on the seventh floor, I will. We are both from poor families. Why do you think that we are on the seventh floor while the richest of the rich are on the first and second floors?" K'Eto pointed out.

"I don't know. I have never noticed or thought about it. Why?" D'Ato questioned.

"That way, the richest students have the shortest walk to their rooms and to the tornado shelters. Not to forget, that is yet another way they get to remind us that we need to keep running to keep up," K'Eto pointed out.

"Oh yes, being born into an affluent family is such a blessing. Looking at these screens really shows what a blessing it is to be rich. Both rich people and poor people and everyone in between are all dropping dead," T'He concluded.

"So, K'Eto, what is your story about how you got her?" D'Ato asked.

"I earned my scholarship by cleaning the church that my mother left me at. Nobody ever got around to adopting me, so the clergy raised me. They taught me to read by reading the *Holy Book of Ablo*. I learned to count by helping them out with the treasury. I learned music by helping them with the services. I learned what college was like when I helped prepare this dorm for us to move in. By the way, this college hires only enough cleaning staff to clean the first- and second-floor dorm rooms, restrooms, and shower areas. That is why everyone else must maintain their own areas until the last day of class, or at least that is the way it worked out every other year," K'Eto explained.

"So, does that mean that you are here to marry rich?" D'Con asked.

"No, I am here to learn the skills to work at a job that actually allows me to pay my bills and afford not to have to get married," K'Eto answered. "At least, that was the plan when I started college. Today, I don't know. All depends on what happens tomorrow. That is, if there is a tomorrow."

"Well, I don't know about anyone else, but I have gotten sick and tired of hearing how those who can only afford to go to college on a scholarship or two need to apologize for anything," K'Ree said. "After all, my son worked long, hard hours trying to invent something that he called a spyglass in order to be 'given' a scholarship, as if scholarships are given out and not earned. Since I work here as a gardener, the only one who would even look at it was Professor O'Well. He promised that he would do what he could to secure a scholarship for my son. Since I have yet to hear a word about it or from Professor O'Well, I can only assume that my son failed to win his scholarship, which no longer matters, compared to his life."

"Looks like it is my turn to confess. I am here on a scholarship too. Both my older brothers and father are members of the state security forces. That is why I am not on the seventh floor but the fifth. What can I say? Being on the fifth floor is one of many benefits that come with having a family in the security forces," T'He confessed. "Not that anyone has to worry about me spying on anyone anymore."

As T'He made her confession, T'Roo whispered into D'Lir's ear, "So, it was K'Ree's son who invented the spyglass that got our Science class in all that trouble. Should we tell her?"

"No. Some confessions are pointless. Considering that Professor O'Well's whereabouts are now unknown, that would only cause her needless pain, I fear, so no," D'Lir whispered back.

L'Rom came down and stumbled into the room. She was complaining, "The air has gotten too thin to breathe, too thin to breathe! I waited and waited, but not a peep or a whisper after the gardener came."

"So whatever has affected the surface has worked its way down to you," D'Con started to say.

"Hold it! Hold it! Look again. We all are beginning to have problems breathing, but none of our bodies are swelling up. There is something different about this," D'Lir said.

"Well, either way, close the door behind her. Maybe, just maybe, we can buy ourselves some more time. We do have security forces, and we do have the All-Powerful and Almighty God and Father, Ablo, who will not let us all die!" D'Con said in her attempt to maintain order.

"Nothing personal, but if this is some part of some greater plan, I wish, I hope, I pray that Our Holy God and Blessed Father, Ablo, will let us in on it before we all die," D'Li said.

*   *   *

Another messenger stumbled into the castle. He said, "Your, Highness, I beg to report. This thinning of the air is spreading. All of our prayers have yet to take effect. Is there nothing that can be done?"

"Yes, so you realized that it is here now. I was going to go into the cellar to continue my prayers for Jeho to save us from whatever horror that Norhem has brought onto us," the king said as he led the way to the basement.

As they walked down the many stairs to the basement, they began to catch their breath, so the messenger asked, "What is this place? I never knew it was here."

"I am not surprised. Most people do not know about this place. Once upon a time, it was the dungeon, where only the most dangerous of criminals were held. But then one of my predecessors—I forget which one—thought on the matter and realized that housing the most dangerous convicts so close to the seat of the government was an invitation to danger. So he had another dungeon built as far away from here as he could. That is why the dungeon is now on a secluded island on the far side of So'hem. But since you can't destroy a dungeon without destroying the foundations, the dungeon was abandoned for a long time, until my father, King A'Mar XIX, reopened it and made it his personal tornado shelter and wine cellar. As you can see, I keep only the finest of the So'hemian wines. I find that the best wines come from the near southern regions. In addition, you can see that I also have invested in several security cameras, but only a few, since I prefer to find out what my enemies are up to face to face. After all, hidden cameras do not show everything, and you cannot ask them any questions."

The effects began to hit the castle of So'hem's King A'Mar XX Shra, where he had retreated to his cellar.

"If this place is that top secret, Your Highness, then should I be here?" the messenger questioned.

"Desperate times call for desperate measures," King A'Mar responded. His words prompted the memory of his firstborn child. A messenger told a much younger King A'Mar that his queen was about to give birth. The royal doctor was coming to the royal palace to deliver the child but then showed him that this child, this girl child, would grow up to have the red eyes and blue hair of a Norhemian, marking her a far better spy than a princess. However, this could only be done if everyone else in So'hem believed that the queen had miscarried while the queen and her nurses secretly cared for the newborn. Today that very same royal father now wondered, *How is she? Where is she? Is she still alive? Does she really understand why I raised her up to become a spy? If not, could she forgive me? Did she forgive me? Does she remember that I not only snuck peeks at her but also kissed away a tear a time or two? Does she know that I never stopped loving her, even though at the time of her birth, desperate times called for desperate measures, and the best thing that the king of So'hem could do was to turn his family's personal curse into a public blessing for the good of all So'hem?*

"Your Highness, you were saying?" the messenger said.

"Where was I? Oh, yes. As I was about to say, fear not. Should we live to tell about this, I can always have you beheaded," the king responded, laughing loudly. He walked over to the far wall and turned on various screens.

"Oh, how comforting," the messenger said, not knowing what else to say.

"Speaking of comfort, pick a bottle any bottle and open it, that is, if you know how to use a corkscrew, and pour us each glass," the king commanded.

CHAPTER 14

THE PRIME MINISTER'S DUNGEON

"Hold on! What is happening up there? Or should I say, what is not happening up there? There should have been a changing of the guards at least an hour ago. There should be someone coming down to feed the prisoners. Why isn't that happening?" Prime Minister E'Li questioned, barely able to talk after his body has swollen up yet again. He continued to sit on the ground, leaning against the dungeon door, all of his joints too painful to move and no longer able to stand. That not only holds the professor prisoner but keeps the prisoner able to see the prime minister's condition. He no longer cared how dirty he had gotten or would get.

"Yes, that is you, your government and your church. Don't bother to ask why we are suffocating or why the other prisoners have given up their fight for their lives so quickly and so readily. Just look at those guards from a distance and imagine that they are asleep on duty as if they did not die in their sleep," Professor O'Well said, he too barely able to breathe or move.

"That is because of your faith in man's science. But our faith is in Our Blessed Holy God and Blessed Father, Ablo, our all-powerful, all-mighty, and all-loving God and Father, Ablo, who will not let Norhem die!" the prime minister explained as he continued to fight even harder just to breathe.

"I don't believe this. No matter what is going on all around you, you can still collapse on the ground, sit there, and claim that there is no science to what is happening to us. This is what happens when the state religion claims to have all the answers and we are forbidden to ask any questions. That is what science is all about, asking questions and more questions. Yet here we are, we have got to be living out the reality of how gravity, electricity, and magnetism are all connected to each other, somehow, someway that the *Holy Book of Ablo* said should not be happening but is. Questions once forbidden to ask—their answers are now our death sentence. We must have used the one to nearly destroy the other two, if not thoroughly weaken, to such a degree that we no longer have air to breathe. But there you are, claiming that Ablo will save us. If Our Holy God and Blessed Father, Ablo, is going to preserve us, he needs to hurry up. I fear we may be some of the last survivors of Norhem," Professor O'Well said.

"So, in the end, all that will be left of Archadea will be So'hem and their kind," the prime minister said sadly.

"Yes, here come your priorities yet again. You do realize that Norhem has only just begun to self-destruct, and once Norhem does self-destruct, then there will be no safe place on this entire planet of Archadea. It may take So'hem more time to die, but what happens here will eventually affect there and everywhere," Professor O'Well explained. "Are you still there?"

"Yes, I am still here. You are not getting rid of me that easily. Nor will So'hem get rid of us this easily. By Ablo's Grace, Norhem will rise again," the prime minister exclaimed as he lost his battle to keep breathing.

"So, you still refuse to understand or to acknowledge that this is one thing that Ablo cannot save us from. She cannot save us from ourselves. The other thing is that So'hem did not do this to us. We did this to ourselves—and maybe to them too," Professor O'Well explained as he too surrendered to suffocation.

* * *

Meanwhile, at the king's castle in So'hem, King A'Mar sat at his roundtable along with the messenger, drinking wine.

He said, "I don't understand. I don't believe it. How can this be?" as they too began to gasp for air as they watched Norhem get sucked into space, piece by piece and as one screen after another faded to black.

"Your Highness, does this mean the final conflict between good and evil is finally happening? If so, where is the victory that Jeho promised us? He is the great and mighty True God of gods. How could he go down to defeat to that false god, that demon in disguise of theirs?" the messenger questioned as he continued to gasp for air.

"I don't know, but I fear we will find that out soon enough. After all, it does feel as if we are only moments away from being called by Jeho to his heaven for our judgment. I hope to be found worthy, as I hope you are too," the king said. "Letitbeso."

"Letitbeso," the messenger said in agreement as both men placed their heads on the table and gave up their fight to stay alive.

EPILOGUE

Eventually, even those in the underground shelters surrendered to suffocation until there was not a breathing soul left on Archaea. Slowly in Archadean time but all too quickly in cosmic time, eventually, not only all their buildings and their people were blown through into the vacuum of space, but even their rivers, lakes, and oceans evaporated into space. Over time, this freeze-drying caused Archaea to shrink to a fraction of the size it once was, that is, when it had a magnetic field that protected its atmosphere and was large enough to hold onto its main moon. The moon has since drifted off into space, and its whereabouts are unknown. But at least one of the garden stones that was covered in mud and in Edelweiss landed on the blue planet, soon to be named Earth. There, it struck a landmass, where the white edelweiss flowers would continue to bloom and to grow. But not everything was all rosy about that. By striking this planet as it did, it triggered a meteorite shower that destroyed many a city-state to the south of that strike. Those meteorites destroyed several city-states, including both Sodom and Gomorrah, thus inspiring fear and intolerance of other religions.

Printed in the United States
By Bookmasters